It came so ... surprise for an instant. A gun began flashing not fifty yards ahead of the lead mule, and slightly off the trail, where a salt hummock, crowned with tenacious brush, offered a hide-out. The stuffed Mackinaw jacket jerked to the impact of two bullets, and Kelly heard the vicious scream of one past his ear.

Then he was shooting back with the Henry. The mules, panicked by the gunfire, swerved violently off the trail, and the wagon went up on two wheels. It hung there an instant, but righted itself. Kelly sawed the mules to a stop and sensed that two more bullets had torn through the canvas top past him.

He leaped from the wagon. Against the background of alkali he knew he was a fair target, but he wanted to draw the fire on himself, away from the girl and Bud Emerson and from the team. He was moving, zigzagging as he ran. The ambusher's gun kept flaming. Kelly heard slugs pass him, and one kicked up the alkali at his feet.

There was no question that the hidden man was armed with a pistol. And there was no doubt that Dunk Tipton was doing the shooting. Tipton was a pistol expert.

Kelly was moving. He ran toward that hummock, which proved to be some twenty yards or more across. Tipton was on the opposite side of the hummock. Kelly abandoned his own rifle now, knowing that the finish of this would be at close quarters....

CLIFF FARRELL

THE WHITE FEATHER

LEISURE BOOKS   NEW YORK CITY

A LEISURE BOOK®

March 2005

Published by special arrangement with Golden West Literary Agency.

Dorchester Publishing Co., Inc.
200 Madison Avenue
New York, NY 10016

ISBN 0-8439-5518-X

Printed in the United States of America.

Visit us on the web at www.dorchesterpub.com.

Table of Contents

Foreword

Cliff Farrell was the author of twenty-five well-reviewed and popular Western novels published over a twenty-three year period, beginning with *Follow the New Grass* (Random House, 1954). But by the time that first book was published, Farrell had already been writing for nearly thirty years and had published close to six hundred stories in a wide variety of markets ranging from pulp fiction magazines to *The Saturday Evening Post*. During much of this same period, Farrell maintained a successful career as a newspaper editor and writer.

Alfonso Clifford Farrell was born in Zanesville, Ohio on November 20, 1899. From an early age he was fascinated by the newspaper world, and worked at the local newspaper while still in high school. After graduation, while still in his teens, he held the position of city editor on a newspaper in Canton, Ohio. Shortly afterward he worked his way westward from Ohio to California, jumping from one newspaper job to another. By his mid-twenties he was night news editor and sports news editor for the Los Angeles *Examiner*. To supplement his newspaper salary, he began submitting short stories to the pulp fiction magazines. The first story failed to find a buyer, but the second, dealing with auto racing — an area he was covering at the moment in his newspaper work — was accepted by Street & Smith's *Sport Story* magazine. Nearly a hundred stories followed, most dealing with sports and auto racing. By 1926 Farrell had branched out into other fields, including Westerns, which would become his main interest.

His first Western stories appeared in *Cowboy Stories* in

1926 under the byline A. Clifford Farrell. Starting in 1931, the byline was shortened to Cliff Farrell. However, for some reason, during the eight years (1928-1935) during which he sold stories to Street & Smith's *Wild West Weekly*, all of his stories in that magazine appeared under one or another of the three "house names" Philip F. Deere, Frank J. Litchfield, or Nels Anderson.

Throughout the 1930s Farrell averaged nearly thirty published stories a year, many of them of novella length. The high point of productivity was reached in 1936, with thirty-six published stories. In a list of "the tops in pulp paper writers" published in *The Writer's 1937 Yearbook*, Farrell shared the honors with Max Brand, Erle Stanley Gardner, Walt Coburn, Murray Leinster, and others. During the 1940s Farrell continued to appear in the Western pulps with both new and reprinted stories, but his markets also expanded to include general circulation magazines such as *The Saturday Evening Post*, *Liberty*, *Country Gentleman*, *Woman's Day*, and the *Star Weekly*, the magazine supplement of the Toronto *Star* newspaper.

Having decided to turn his attention to book-length works, Farrell had only a handful of shorter works published during the 1950s. He wrote his first book-length story, *Follow the New Grass*, in 1952. It was rewritten twice during the next two years, and an abridged version was published in the August 1953 issue of *Zane Grey's Western Magazine* under the title "The Pitchfork Boss". Random House published the book in 1954, and a second novel, *West With the Missouri*, the following year. Two further novels were published as paperback originals by Popular Library. Then, with *Santa Fe Wagon Boss* in 1958, Farrell began a nineteen-year association with Doubleday, for whose Double-D Western imprint he produced a novel each year — with an extra one in 1960 and again in 1965. Most of his books were book-club selections and were also reprinted in paperback form, reaching a wide and appreciative audience.

From time to time during his writing career, Farrell returned to newspaper work, first at the Los Angeles *Examiner* and later at the Los Angeles *Times*. But as he told friends, he felt that the fun and excitement had gone out of newspaper work. It was much more satisfying to stay at his home in Mar Vista, with easy access to the swimming and fishing that he loved, or, with Mildred, his wife of more than thirty years, to indulge a love of travel, both in the American West and in Europe and Africa. Farrell had always been concerned with historical and geographical accuracy in his work, and this lifelong interest finally bore fruit in his next-to-last book, and only work of non-fiction, *The Mighty Land* (Doubleday, 1975).

Cliff Farrell died on November 5, 1977, after a brief illness.

All of the traditional plots and perils of Western fiction — wagon trains, cattle drives, rustling, land grabs, attacks by Indians or by outlaw bands, fistfights, gunfights — appear in Farrell's fiction, always described with vividness and economy. The disgraced family member or unjustly accused loner, struggling to find or reclaim a place in society, is a common figure in many stories. Farrell is especially good at distinguishing a character quickly through speech and small details of dress and manner. The fight scenes are vivid, and even the most breathless action is clearly and efficiently set forth. But the single most noticeable characteristic of Farrell's writing, apparent in almost every story he produced, is his emotional investment in his characters. He cared about them, and so does the reader.

R. E. Briney

Sign of the White Feather

"Sign of the White Feather" borrows the "white feather" symbol of cowardice from A. E. W. Mason's well-known 1902 novel. Here the recipient is Kelly Brackett, the son of the owner of a logging company in Utah during the Civil War. The company is competing to supply poles for the Western leg of a crucial telegraph line. Kelly's refusal to fight when challenged by a competing company's bully boy, and his lack of explanation for his actions, earn him the disdain of family and enemies alike. The lingering effects of an old feud between Kelly's father and a former partner provide additional complications. The story was completed in July, 1945 and sold in November of that year to the Trojan Publishing's line of fiction pulps. It was published as the lead story in the March, 1946 issue of *Fighting Western*.

I

"WESTBOUND STAGE"

The westbound stage was two hours behind schedule, and Kelly Brackett had offered the driver a dollar for every minute of the time he made up over the remaining fifty miles into Salt Lake City. The driver evidently needed the money. The trail was a devil's nest of chuckholes and rock jawbreakers that tested the strength of the leather thorough braces. The eight passengers, jammed inside to escape the chill wind of early September that drove down from the high slopes of the Wasatch Mountains, were being battered to a state of raw, protesting nerves as they clung to the arm slings and to each other in the bouncing vehicle.

Kelly shared the forward seat with a blocky man named Sid Nelson and a gaunt-framed Mormon bishop who had shoulders as square and unyielding as a hay rake. Kelly's own shoulders were far from puny. He weighed one hundred and eighty-five, but looked many pounds lighter. His coat had needed no padding, as a fashionable tailor had discovered when fitting him in St. Louis a fortnight previously.

He tried to wedge himself in a corner, and clenched his teeth in an attempt to offset the pile-driving pain that streaked through his head with each jolt. Beneath his pearl-gray, cloth top hat, he bore on his dark-thatched head an angry lump.

It probably had been a blackjack that had glanced off his head when he had strolled into the shadows to take a few puffs from the stub of his last cigar at Fort Bridger during the previous midnight stop. Or it may have been only a rock slung in a neckerchief. All that Kelly was certain about was that someone had swung viciously, and hadn't cared whether or not the blow crushed his skull. More than forty-eight hours previously, a bullet, also from the shadows, had missed him by inches during the stop at Denver City. That bullet might have been an accident or a case of mistaken identity, but the second incident at Fort Bridger had proved that it was neither.

Someone knew, or had guessed correctly, that Kelly's mission to St. Louis had been successful. That person evidently also believed that Kelly was returning West with cash amounting to $30,000 on his person.

14

Kelly wished only that this second assumption was correct. In spite of what had happened back along the trail, his mind would have been more at peace if the money were in his possession. He had reason to believe that it was aboard this stage, but there was a nagging possibility that he had only been played for a sucker. That was one reason why his head ached.

In fact, in spite of his fine broadcloth long-coat, belled gray trousers, and pleated linen in which he had arrayed himself in order to impress the bankers in St. Louis, Kelly was down to his last dollar.

His suede leather poke, which bulged importantly when he flashed it, was weighted with worthless brass tavern checks and copper washers that he had filched here and there. Because of lack of funds he had been forced to forego the pleasure of eating for the past twenty-four hours, and he always had been the possessor of a lusty appetite.

His mood was, therefore, not expansive. The stage bounced high, and he tried to brace himself for the jolt. It came, and his lips twisted in a grimace of agony.

His glance momentarily met the gaze of the only feminine passenger aboard, a prim young lady who sat in the opposite seat between a big, brick-faced Irishman and a mild, little, pious-talking man in a wing collar. Her eyes, gray-green and impersonal, studied him briefly, as though estimating his capacity for absorbing further punishment.

The coach careened over another obstacle with a spine-jarring crash. The young lady, after collecting herself, said plaintively: "Oh, dear!"

She had been saying that same damned thing almost every mile all the way from Atchison. Twelve hundred miles of it. Kelly had never been a patient man. He had heard of the legendary Oriental method of torturing a man with little drops of water. This was what this girl was doing to him — deliberately.

Garbed modestly in gray, with her wheat-gold hair tucked modestly into a severe poke bonnet, she had a resigned but brave voice. It was understood that she was westbound to join some relative. The fortitude with which she had endured the rigors of night-and-day journey across the plains had aroused the protective instincts of every masculine passenger — except Kelly. He would have enjoyed wringing her neck.

The big Irishman had slugged a muleskinner at Medicine Bow for using strong language in her hearing. Smoking had been ruled out inside the coach as a mark of respect to her.

The coach jack-rabbited over another high center. The girl uttered her customary sigh of resignation. She started to frame her favorite expression.

Kelly beat her to the draw. He mimicked her brave voice. "Oh, hell!" he said.

The bishop turned and gave him a reproving look. Sid Nelson, who had been very attentive to the girl, frowned at this startling affront. The husky Irishman bristled. His name was Peter Shanley. Big and horny-handed and ill at ease in a celluloid collar, he had the earmarks of a typical construction crew foreman. Since boarding the stage at Denver, he had taken a fatherly interest in the unescorted young lady, and he was quick now to demonstrate his toughness.

" 'Tis a decent tongue you will keep in your head, young man," he stated, leaning forward. "Or it is myself that will teach you how to conduct yourself in the presence of your betters."

The girl spoke up swiftly. "Please don't bother about poor little me, Mister Shanley. I never hear anything I don't want to hear. It just goes in one ear and out the other." Her voice

16

was sugary; it was a deliberate goad to the Irishman, prodding him into throwing his weight around.

"It is no bother," Shanley assured her as the cumulative tide of red welled up in his face.

"He didn't really mean to be rude," the girl fluttered. "I'm sure he'll be glad to offer an apology."

"Well, me lad," Shanley said significantly. "We're waitin' to hear you beg the young lady's pardon."

Kelly glanced grimly at the girl and saw again that measuring irony in her. He wondered what the Irishman would say if he mentioned that she was traveling under an assumed name, that she was as tough as a boot when it came to financial dealings, and had a mind like a steel trap.

She had seized on Peter Shanley's belligerency with the coolness of a tiger stalking its prey to put Kelly in a position where he would either have to fight or humble himself to her.

Seething helplessly inside, he said: "All right. I apologize, Miss Wells."

The Irishman was disappointed. He slowly sank back into his seat, disgusted.

"Thank you, Mister Brackett, is it?" the girl murmured forgivingly.

Peter Shanley sat up again. "Brackett, is it?" he exclaimed. "By the saints, is it possible that you are Barbas Brackett's son?"

Kelly tightened up. "Yes," he said tersely.

Peter Shanley's rugged face became scornful as he looked Kelly over from head to foot. "So," he sniffed. "I have heard that Barbas Brackett's son turned tail an' ran rather than fight a man that had beaten his own father to a pulp. I have worked for Barbas Brackett, an', whatever else may have been said of him, he, at least, did his own fightin'. I did not believe that one of his flesh and blood would back water. But seein' is believin'."

17

II

"CHICKEN FEATHERS"

Nobody said anything for a time. Kelly could feel sweat on his palms despite the chill temperature, but he remained silent.

Peter Shanley parted a storm curtain and spat over a wheel as though he had tasted something repulsive.

The coach hit another chuckhole, and the girl said maliciously: "Oh, dear!"

Kelly took that in silence, also. He was wondering just where Ellen Lash was carrying the $30,000 she had promised to loan his father — on her own terms and face to face in Salt Lake City; he speculated for the thousandth time on whether she had any money at all, and was merely leading him on a vengeful will-o'-the-wisp path that would wind up in disaster for Brackett & Company.

If she really had the money, he knew now, beyond question, that her terms would be severe. If there was any doubt that she was out to exact every pound of flesh possible from the Bracketts, that doubt had been removed by this latest little humiliation she had arranged for him. He had to concede she was a clever actress. Only a brute would consider such a helpless female worth robbing.

Kelly's mission to St. Louis, necessarily, had become pretty well noised around in financial circles, but he doubted that anyone except themselves knew that it was Ellen Lash who had agreed to put up the money. They had met and closed the deal secretly. For her protection they had pretended no previous acquaintance when they boarded the stage at Atchison. That attitude had not been difficult for Ellen Lash because of her antipathy toward Kelly. For her, at least, the arrangement had proved extremely wise, for it was Kelly who was taking his lumps and being shot at, while she went unmolested.

These two attempts on his life, more than four hundred miles apart, had convinced Kelly that his assailant was a fellow passenger on this stage.

He had been studying the other six men all day. In addition to the Irishman and the Mormon bishop there was a saturnine, olive-skinned man of the tinhorn gambler type who looked capable of any type of skullduggery. Sitting next to the girl was the little, buttery-voiced traveler with the pious manners. His name was Cyrus Vine. Next was the bulky Sid Nelson, bluff, hearty-voiced, who talked importantly of big mining deals and big money. However, he had the fishy eyes and bloated nose of a hard-drinker. Kelly tabbed him as either a lawyer or a confidence man. The remaining passenger in the jump seat was a small-mouthed youth in a linen duster who Kelly labeled as a deserter from some state militia, fleeing West to escape Army duty.

That left Kelly where he had been when that blackjack had stunned him in the darkness alongside the mule corral at Bridger. It might have been any one of these men, or none of them. He had not glimpsed his assailant.

Only Ellen Lash knew he had been slugged. She had happened upon him as he lay there, his mind wool-gathering. She had hurriedly doctored the bruise on his head and got him back on his feet.

Ellen Lash had kept mum about that affair. Kelly surmised that she knew the significance of that episode. She must be fully aware that someone aboard this stage was after

19

the money she was carrying, or meant to see that it never reached Barbas Brackett.

"Weber's Station!" the driver bawled. "Twenty minutes fer grub pile. Elk steak an' side trimmin's. Dollar a throw. Shake a laig, folks."

The stage lurched to a stop and the passengers piled out, flexing cramped muscles. Kelly's head swam for a moment after he got his feet on solid ground. Then he steadied.

The station was a flat-roofed, oblong structure of mud and rock, loopholed as a protection against the Cheyennes. A hostler was bringing a fresh team of matched bays from the barn. Chickens and hogs had the run of the place.

The chatter of a telegraph sounder drifted from a room at the east end of the station. Until a few weeks previously it had been a Pony Express office, but the wooden sign over the door had been freshly painted over and now bore the name of the Pacific Telegraph Company.

Overhead, new copper wire gleamed in the wan sun. It marched up the cañon from the direction of Salt Lake, and strode onward from pole to pole eastward toward the construction camp that had advanced beyond Bridger. There men were stringing wire and setting poles with relentless haste, moving onward to meet a similar crew that was advancing westward from Fort Kearney to meet them.

West of Salt Lake where Overland Telegraph had the franchise for linking the Mormon capital with Carson City, Jim Gamble's wire stringers were engaged in a similar race to close the gap through the dreary wastes of the Paiute country before winter put an end to construction work.

It was out in Nevada that Kelly's black-jowled, hard-fisted father had taken on the toughest job of his career when he contracted with Overland Telegraph to cut and deliver ten thousand peeled poles, twenty-six feet in length, from the high parks of the wild Ruby Mountains.

Self-sufficient, self-made, and willful, Barbas Brackett had consulted no one when he signed that contract. Least of all had he considered asking help from his son who he had disowned. Now he lay helpless in Salt Lake, nursing crushed ribs, a broken leg, and other injuries that he had sustained in a fight with a treacherous, slab-muscled foreman named Mike Hatch.

His own son had dealt the ultimate blow to his pride by refusing to meet that same Mike Hatch in physical combat. Barbas Brackett was not accustomed to defeat. He never asked quarter, nor offered it, either in brawls or in business affairs. Until he met Mike Hatch he had never met a man he couldn't whip. And he had ruthlessly smashed more than one rival in the construction and logging business who had the temerity to cross his path.

Now he was facing ruination. He had strained his resources to the limit to move crews and equipment across the plains and into the unexplored Rubies. He had taken a gambler's chance when he agreed to take stock in Overland Telegraph instead of cash upon completion of the contract. He believed the stock would make him a millionaire in the future.

He had made his first error of judgment when he underestimated the temper of the Southern states. Barbas Brackett had believed that the secessionist trouble would blow over. But Bull Run had now been fought and Mr. Lincoln was calling for more volunteers.

In the financial chaos following the outbreak of the war, a bank in which Barbas Brackett's cash reserve was deposited had closed its doors, leaving him without means of meeting his payrolls.

He had made his second mistake when he borrowed $25,000 on a ninety-day note from a cold-jawed financier in

San Francisco named Luther Pritchard. He had put up all his assets as security, including this contract with Overland Telegraph. Barbas Brackett had expected to complete his logging job long before that note came due, and to pay off the obligation with money he could raise on the stock he was to receive. But that note now fell due at midnight.

But, with only a scant few hours of grace remaining, the logging was barely half completed. Whiskey peddlers had debauched his men, troublemakers incited strikes and slow-downs. Mike Hatch, ringleader of the troublemakers, had beaten Barbas Brackett in a bloody battle when Barbas Brackett fired him. Hatch had put the boots to his victim, leaving him broken in body, if not in spirit.

Hatch had promised the same done to Barbas Brackett's son, but Kelly had taken the next stage East. Now, he was on his way back to the scene of his disgrace.

Kelly stood there, savoring the aroma of food from the dining room. He watched Sid Nelson gallantly squire Ellen Lash toward the door of the eating place.

So it's Nelson that's buying her dinner this time, Kelly reflected sullenly. He doubted if Ellen Lash had opened her purse all the way from Atchison. Some male passenger had invariably been dazzled into escorting her to the table at every stop. She had even used her wiles on the Mormon bishop to gain free food. The gambler and the baby-faced kid and Kelly were the only ones she hadn't bothered to charm.

Kelly's stomach rolled and he ran the back of his hand over his mouth. He was wolf-hungry, but he didn't have the price of a full meal, and he did not want Ellen Lash to learn the extent of his poverty.

The blaze of a trumpet sounded. He watched a column of mounted men approach on the trail, coming from the west.

"It is recruits they are for Abe Lincoln's Army," Peter Shanley boomed approvingly. "Now ain't they the brave lads?"

The contingent came riding past, led by a man wearing officer's insignia, who saluted the Stars and Stripes which hung from the station staff. The group of stage passengers cheered and Ellen Lash clapped gloved hands.

Some of the eastbound volunteers were partly outfitted in Union uniforms, but the majority wore homespun and hide boots.

Kelly's natty attire drew the critical interest of one beardless recruit on a bony buckskin horse. "You're headin' in the wrong direction, ain't you, mister?" the rider jeered. "The Johnny Rebs air back thar . . . thet other way."

"Use your head, Butch," another hooted. "That finefeathered rooster knows which direction the Rebs air. Else why would he be makin' tracks West?"

Kelly had read about people who wished the ground would open and swallow them. Now he knew just how they felt. He fought the panicky impulse to turn and flee from sight. But there was no escape. He forced himself to stand there and take it. He felt nauseated. There was torture in his eyes, and all the color had drained out of his face. His eyes were like his father's, with latent storm in their dark depths, but his features were those of his mother — sensitive, highstrung, well-bred.

Ellen Lash left the group at the dining room door, and paused to pick up a white chicken feather from the ground. Kelly knew what she was going to do as she confronted him. Her gray-green eyes were ironic, vengeful.

Momentarily she had abandoned her rôle as a frail flower. She was not a tall girl, but she was well-formed, sturdy. Her eyes were wide-spaced above full cheek bones and a nose that

23

turned up challengingly. She was not beautiful by any standard. But she had these other men falling over themselves to serve her.

She thrust the white feather into a buttonhole on Kelly's coat lapel. "You seem to go well with that color," she remarked.

The recruits cheered wildly and raised a bedlam of catcalls for Kelly's benefit.

"You're overdoing things," Kelly murmured. "You're letting your malice show. First thing you know somebody will suspect that you're not all you pretend."

Ellen Lash was pleased by the fury in his face. She gave him a mocking curtsy, then moved with her easy, swinging walk back to where Sid Nelson waited. She placed her hand daintily on the man's arm and went into the eating room.

The Army volunteers rode on past, heading for a night's bivouac in the sagebrush beyond the station. The stage travelers filed into the dining room, grinning over their shoulders at Kelly. He stood there alone wearing that white chicken feather.

III

"ROBBIE"

Kelly walked into the telegraph office. Scribbling a message, he handed it to a lank operator who had a prominent Adam's apple, a lump of tobacco in his jaw, and wore a drooping mustache.

The operator insultingly eyed the white feather that Kelly carried stubbornly where Ellen Lash had placed it. The man then indolently began counting the words in the message. His interest quickened, and he scanned it a second time.

Miss Roberta McDowell,
c/o Overland Telegraph,
Salt Lake City
   Will arrive on evening stage. I like my fatted calf with just a touch of garlic sauce. Love and kisses.

Kelly Brackett

The operator's watery eyes jerked up and peered curiously at Kelly. "I heard an operator gossipin' on the wire today," he drawled. "He said Mike Hatch was hangin' around Salt Lake, rollin' 'em high."

Kelly placed both hands flat on the counter and looked at the man. "That information is free, I take it," he said levelly. "But is there any charge on the message? If so, send it collect."

The operator backed away suddenly. He hastily seated himself at the table and began rattling the brass. "No charge," he mumbled. "Courtesy of Pacific Telegraph to Overland. But don't say I didn't warn yuh."

Kelly said: "You give service, don't you?" He turned then and strolled outside. An eastbound stage had just pulled in and was disgorging passengers, who were straggling toward the eating room.

One of the arrivals came heading toward Kelly at almost a run. His mind far away, Kelly gazed almost unseeingly at this young lady, who was holding her skirts clear of the dust in her hurry.

"Kelly!" she was exclaiming.

"Robbie," he responded mechanically. Then he aroused with a start. "Robbie! You witch! I just sent you a wire, and now you're here in person. I thought I was dreaming. So you ride your broomstick even in daytime?"

To the amazement of the onlookers he lifted her high, set her down again. Then he kissed her lustily. He would have kept right on kissing her, but Roberta McDowell, laughing a little, pulled away from him.

"People are watching," she reproved.

Kelly glanced at the ring she wore on the third finger of her left hand. It was a heavy, masculine ring, but it was all that he had handy when he had placed it on her finger more than two months in the past.

"Let 'em look." He grinned. "I haven't seen you for a month, you know. What are you doing here?"

"I couldn't wait. I got your pony letter from Atchison and knew you should be on today's stage, so I came out this far to meet you."

Roberta McDowell was listed on the payroll as Barbas Brackett's secretary. She was more than that. She had been with the company since she was nineteen, and Kelly had been asking her to marry him almost since the first time he had met her.

She was now the balance wheel of Brackett & Company. She was the only person Barbas Brackett implicitly trusted, the only one who could handle him when he was in one of his black rages. He had said more than once that fate had played a dirty trick on him when it had given him a spineless son instead of a daughter like Robbie.

She was a straight-legged, alluring young woman of nearly twenty-four now. A tight-fitting plaid jacket molded to her sure lines. A chip hat was perched on her hair, which was thick and well-brushed, with the light picking out golden shadows in its deep amber coils. Her eyes, too, were amber, and self-possessed.

"Lord, you're pretty," Kelly said worshipfully.

Her mouth smiled, but he saw a question — and a doubt in her eyes. His elation faded.

He led her out of earshot of any prying listeners. He hadn't forgotten those two attempts on his life and that at least one person probably was watching every move he made. He discovered that his fingers were shaking. Not wanting her to perceive just how moved he was by her nearness, he reluctantly released her arm. What he really wanted to do was to hold Robbie McDowell tightly against him and drive that doubt out of her eyes — out of her mind, and out of her heart.

"Did you get the money, Kelly?" she asked tensely.

"I think it will arrive safely in Salt Lake," he said. "Gosh, Robbie, I still can't believe you're really here. I've been. . . ."

"You *think* so? Oh, Kelly! Aren't you sure . . . about the money, I mean?"

Kelly didn't want to talk about practical things. He only wanted to talk about Robbie and himself. "The person who promised to make the loan is aboard the stage." He shrugged. "I'm sure of that, at least."

"Who is he, Kelly? Why all this mystery? Your letter was very vague. I've been wiring you at every station this side of Bridger, but you haven't answered. Was it the Pioneer Bank that finally agreed to help us out? They've always been friendly to Brackett and Company."

"I tried the Pioneer." Kelly shrugged again. "But it was no soap. They got hit hard by the panic in the cotton market, like a lot of other banks. I applied at every other place I could think of. I put up a big front. See these duds I'm wearing? I tried to put over the idea that Brackett and Company wasn't as broke as it really is. It didn't work. They acted like I had smallpox. I didn't fool anybody. They all knew as much about Brackett and Company as I did. The word had gone around. Luther Pritchard saw to that. And nobody was at all keen about bucking Pritchard. He swings too big a club."

"You're still dodging the question," Robbie charged, nettled. "Who finally promised us the loan?"

Kelly hesitated. "Ellen Lash," he said reluctantly.

Robbie's mouth popped open. "Ellen Lash?" she echoed. "Not . . . not *the* Ellen Lash?"

"There's only one of that name that I know," Kelly said. He added fervently: "Thank the good Lord."

"You couldn't," Robbie said, bewildered. "It's . . . it's insane. Why her father hated Barbas Brackett to his dying day. He swore on his deathbed he'd come back and haunt Barbas."

"Something tells me a chain-clanking ghost would be a pushover in comparison to handling Ellen Lash in the flesh," Kelly said wryly. "I'd settle for the ghost right now."

"I'm the one that must be dreaming," Robbie said. "Ellen Lash would be the last person in the world who'd offer help to. . . ."

"Well, she was the last person in Saint Louis who would take a chance on Brackett and Company." Kelly nodded. "When a drowning man finds a rope thrown into his hand, he doesn't fritter away his time trying to find out what's at the other end. I had to grab, and grab quick."

"You actually went to Ellen Lash and asked her to loan money to your father?"

"No. I wasn't that bright. It was her idea entirely. I received a note at my hotel suggesting that, if I was interested in discussing a certain business proposition, that I might find it worthwhile to call at a certain address. The house proved to be in a respectable residential district. The note had not been signed, but Ellen Lash had sent it. She was there, expecting me."

"Well, of all things."

"We closed the deal over a cup of tea. I watched closely to make sure she didn't poison the tea. I'm still alive, so I presume she'll get around to that little detail some other time."

"Ellen Lash actually volunteered to loan thirty thousand dollars to your father?"

"Robbie, you're beautiful, even with your mouth open. But you're attracting attention. Wipe that stunned look off your pretty face. Ellen Lash laid it out cold. She would kick in with cash on her own terms. And she didn't intend entrusting it to any low-down Brackett person to take it to Salt Lake. She said she would see to it that it got there safely . . . in her possession." Kelly added tersely: "It wasn't hard to guess that she wants the pleasure of facing Barbas Brackett personally. She isn't a forgiving person. I'm afraid she's going to rub the salt in plenty deep. I had to agree. Time is running short."

"Where would she get that much money?" Robbie demanded skeptically.

"I didn't ask her personally. You don't usually look a gift horse in the mouth. But I had Bill North at Pioneer make a few discreet inquiries. He learned that Ellen Lash hadn't been left penniless by any means. She had inherited the house she was living in and a few other pieces of property. It seems that she had just closed a deal for all her property, making the price cheap for a quick cash sale."

"What if she backs out at the last minute?" Robbie said, worried.

"That chance" — Kelly shrugged — "is one I had to take. It's been keeping me awake nights, too." He added reflectively: "I've known Ellen Lash since I was in knee pants. She's detested me every minute of her life. It's been bred into her. I've guessed that it dates back to her father's time, but I've never heard the exact details as to why she sees red every time a Brackett crosses her path. Do you happen to know why?"

Robbie bit her lip and showed signs of wanting to change the subject.

"Speak up," Kelly insisted. "I have no illusions regarding my father's character. Did he hit below the belt, or did he use an axe on someone named Lash?"

"I heard the story from an old construction man," Robbie said reluctantly. "Kendall Lash and your father were partners when they were young men and just starting out in the lumber business. Unfortunately they also fell in love with the same girl. They finally fought it out with their fists. Barbas Brackett won that fight, but the girl married Kendall Lash anyway."

"I see," Kelly said grimly. "And Barbas Brackett didn't take it like a man."

"He never forgave either Kendall Lash or the girl," Robbie admitted. "The partnership ended, of course, and they formed separate companies. Your father hounded Kendall Lash mercilessly, underbid him at every chance, and finally drove him out of business. Kendall Lash hated Barbas Brackett to the day of his death, ten years ago. Ellen Lash's mother is dead, too. She died the day Ellen was born."

"Knowing Barbas Brackett better than any person alive," Kelly said slowly, "I can believe that story."

The stage driver, impatient to win the bonus Kelly had offered, was shouting: "Time's up, folks! We're hittin' the trail. Hurry it up!"

Robbie, who had been so occupied with other things, now began staring at the white feather. "What's that?" she demanded.

Kelly took it from the buttonhole, inspected it thoughtfully, then placed it carefully in a pocket.

"A little souvenir of the occasion, presented to me by Ellen Lash."

"What a nasty little cat she must be. What right . . . ?"

"I'm heading West while other fighting men are going East to join the Army," Kelly reminded her.

"That young lady ought to be told that Abraham Lincoln himself has asked that the telegraph line to California be completed before winter if it is humanly possible. Mister Lincoln knows that it will help keep California bound more closely to the Union, and he needs all the help he can get."

"Abe Lincoln needs help in a few other places, too," Kelly remarked. "In Virginia, for instance."

"All the battles aren't going to be fought in Virginia in this war," Robbie asserted.

"I believe I know what you mean," Kelly said solely. "I've been told that Mike Hatch is still waiting in Salt Lake City."

He was watching Robbie and saw the way her glance suddenly refused to meet his eyes.

"Is that the real reason why Ellen Lash pinned that white feather on you?" she demanded.

"Maybe. She didn't say. I couldn't say whether she knows about Mike Hatch or not. But she seems to know a lot about Brackett and Company."

"But that's . . . that's unfair. You didn't have any chance to fight Mike Hatch. If you hadn't taken the stage East that day, you would have had to wait a week. Time was too valuable. You would never have got the money in time to have helped finish the job."

Kelly studied her. "Do you really believe that, Robbie?"

"Of course!" Robbie was emphatic about it — a trifle too emphatic.

"But in your heart you think I took the easiest way out?" Kelly said bitterly.

"I think nothing of the kind," Robbie denied irritably. "We all know Hatch is only a thug, hired by Luther Pritchard to delay the logging so that Barbas Brackett will have to for-

31

feit on that loan. There is no point in fighting a man like Hatch. Anyway, I know you could take care of yourself against that ugly brute."

"I only wish I was so sure of that," Kelly said. Then he dropped that subject. "What's the situation up in the Rubies? How's Barbas Brackett?"

"Your father is recovering. He's able to cuss now, and is getting around on crutches a little. But his leg is still in splints. He won't be on his own feet for weeks, at least. And the job has come to almost a complete standstill, Kelly. We're sunk unless we get fast action."

"Bring me up to date on the situation."

"Things have gone from bad to worse. Word got around that Brackett and Company was about broke. Luther Pritchard took care of that. When we couldn't meet our last payroll, nearly all of the loggers quit the camp and came into Salt Lake. Only a few of the old-timers who've been with Barbas Brackett for years are still in the Rubies, and they can't do much. Jim Gamble is frantic. His crews are almost out of poles, and they've still got more than a hundred miles of wire to string."

"Who's been in charge of the men since I left?"

"Lee Galvin. He's done the best he could, but everything was against him."

Kelly was silent a moment, thinking about the quickness with which Robbie had offered an excuse for Lee Galvin. He said: "Lee isn't a logger. He's a damned good man, a fighter from taw, but he doesn't know timber. He didn't happen to lock horns with Mike Hatch, did he?"

Robbie gave him another of her swift, appraising looks that he was beginning to expect whenever the subject of Mike Hatch was mentioned. "Lee would have fought Hatch," she said, choosing her words carefully. "But I've managed to reason with him. He isn't one of . . . ," she broke off, realizing she had led herself into a blind alley in spite of her caution.

". . . one of the family," Kelly put in for her, and nodded. "It wasn't his father that Hatch beat up. It really isn't Lee Galvin's fight, is it?"

"No," Robbie said, finally cornered. "It isn't."

There it was, stark and uncompromising. Robbie was still wearing his ring, but Kelly knew that deep inside her she was ashamed of it.

The stage driver was imploring: "Last call! Shake a laig, folks. All aboard!"

Robbie looked at the gray-clad girl who was being helped into the coach. "It's Ellen Lash, sure enough," she conceded, as though she still could hardly believe it. "If you ask me, I'd make you a little bet that she'll make Barbas pay plenty for the use of any money she loans . . . if she's really bringing any with her. She'll ask twelve percent. Maybe fifteen."

"What would Barbas Brackett ask if he was in her place?" Kelly asked sardonically. They were moving toward the coach now. "Pretend that you don't know her," he whispered. "She's traveling under the name of Matilda Wells."

"Why?"

There was no time to tell about that bruise on his head and the gun play at Denver. "Just do as I say," Kelly insisted.

He was wondering if the person, or persons, who had engineered the Denver and Bridger incidents would show their hand again before the coach reached its destination. In any event he did not want to let the cat out of the bag now, after having played the rôle of a decoy for Ellen Lash thus far.

He nudged his cap-and-ball pistol, which hung in a shoulder holster, around to where it could be reached quickly. The weight of the gun was comforting, but the real-

33

ization that Salt Lake was less than five hours away was an even greater comfort to him.

He helped Robbie into the rear seat alongside Ellen Lash. In accordance with stagecoach custom they offered self-introductions, but they did not shake hands.

Kelly saw them measure each other with the critical attention for detail with which two attractive women always meet. Ellen Lash's hand went to a loose strand of her fair hair that had escaped the confinement of her prim bonnet, and she tucked it in place. Kelly found a measure of satisfaction in that. Ellen Lash, for all her single-minded purpose, had her share of single-minded vanity. She was finding herself at a disadvantage, with her demure garb and severe bonnet contrasting pointedly with Robbie's fetching and strictly feminine attire.

"You look rather tired, Miss Wells," Robbie said, quick to make the best of her superiority. "I imagine it has been a very trying journey."

"Everyone has been very helpful to me," Ellen Lash said, lowering her eyelashes in Sid Nelson's direction. "I haven't found the trip too wearisome. I am probably a little tired, but then I never was very strong."

Kelly glowered. She was lying in her teeth, he reflected sourly. In his opinion, she had endured the journey far better than the rest of the supposedly tougher males. He believed she was as able to take care of herself, particularly in the clinches, as she had been at the start — and that was plenty.

Kelly himself was feeling the ache of every mile and every jolt of that long journey riding in his bones. He braced himself in his place again and wished he had thought to borrow the price of a meal from Robbie. The pleasure of having her with him had driven his hunger out of his mind, but now it was back again, and his head was giving him hell.

The fresh team took off like a thunderbolt, and pain began to punch through him with each jolt. He remembered that he would have to borrow money to pay the bonus he had offered the ambitious driver. He wanted to sleep twenty-four hours somewhere, then sleep some more. He wanted to tell Robbie a lot of things, make her understand.

He thought of Lee Galvin, the black-haired, hot-eyed assistant to Barbas Brackett. He remembered how quick Robbie had been to exonerate Galvin of responsibility in the matter of Mike Hatch. Kelly tried not to admit it, but he was aware of a dull, hopeless jealousy. He knew instinctively that Lee Galvin was perhaps the biggest answer to that question and doubt that Robbie had shown him when he kissed her.

The stage jostled its way down an interminable cañon, with the wheels groaning on the rocky, gooseneck curves. Bleak rock escarpments shut off the waning daylight, and the chill temperature worked its way into the passengers.

Peering through slits in the storm curtains, Kelly got occasional glimpses of snow-clad peaks in the distance. Winter had come in the high country. It would be coming, also, in the Rubies, three hundred miles farther west. But the snow-line, here in the Wasatch Range at least, was still above 8,000 feet, he estimated. That was probably an accurate gauge of conditions in the Rubies, also.

Sooner or later, and probably sooner, snow would blanket the lower reaches of all these mountains. In the Rubies Barbas Brackett had set up his logging camp at the 5,000-foot level. It was now a race against the elements as well as against Luther Pritchard.

The driver made a fast relay at Daniel's Station and repeated at Kimball's eleven miles farther on. The swift mountain twilight was rising in a purple flood from the cañons as the stage rumbled onward toward Mountain Dell, the last relay point before Salt Lake.

They were emerging into view of the great basin now, with the early evening lamps of Salt Lake showing faintly at that distance through the purple twilight. The trail dropped into a descending ravine, and presently leveled off through a rocky flat, clumped with stunted cedars. The wheels splashed chill water against the curtains as the coach plunged through a rushing creek.

Then the driver uttered a startled shout. Two gunshots sounded, and the stage halted abruptly on locked wheels.

"All right!" a heavy voice shouted. "Pile out, you passengers, with your hands up!"

"Damn the luck," the driver complained. "It's a hold-up, folks! There goes my bonus. An' I had chopped thirty minutes off the time, too. Better do what they say."

IV

"THEY KNEW WHAT THEY WANTED"

"Oh, dear!" Ellen Lash moaned. She promptly keeled over into the startled arms of Sid Nelson.

Robbie leaned over, slapped her smartly on the cheeks. "Don't be a fool," Robbie said sharply. "Fainting won't do any good. You won't be harmed. They just don't do that in this country. They're after money."

Ellen Lash only whispered and clung tighter to Sid Nelson. "They'll kill me," she whimpered.

Kelly cynically noticed that there were warm spots of anger in her cheeks. Ellen Lash hadn't fainted. She was still playing her rôle, and she was resenting being slapped by Robbie. Kelly suddenly lifted her from Sid Nelson's grasp. "Poor thing," he said. "She's hysterical. I'll help her out." He shouted, for the sake of safety: "We got a fainting woman in here! Hold your fire!"

The gambler and the baby-faced youth were already scrambling out, their arms rigidly above their heads.

Kelly, burdened with Ellen Lash's weight, squeezed through the door.

"Damn you," she breathed angrily in his ear. "Keep your hands off me after this. And tell that pretty friend of yours that, if she ever slaps me again, I'll tear her hair out by the roots."

Kelly reached the ground, and stood her on her feet. Forced to play her rôle, she had to cling to him, burying her face against him.

Four mounted men loomed up in the twilight, shotguns and pistols lifted. "Stay on the box, you," one of them ordered the driver. "Hold them horses."

The hold-up men had gunny sacks over their heads, fitted with eyeholes. Long, oiled slickers concealed them, even to their boots, and they had cotton gloves on their hands. Two of them dismounted and, using their cocked guns as a prod, lined up the passengers. Ellen Lash seized this chance to abandon Kelly's support and turn again to Sid Nelson's protection. The fishy-eyed Nelson seemed properly impressed with this display of her esteem for him.

One masked man began ransacking the pockets of the men. The swarthy gambler, who accepted the situation with indifference, was relieved of a few gold pieces and some cheap jewelry. Pete Shanley was brick red with fury as his poke went into a sack into which the loot was being dropped.

"I slaved two months in Barbas Brackett's logging camp to earn the money, ye' devils!" he raged.

"Keep that flannel mouth of yours shut, you mick," the masked man who seemed to be the leader ordered.

"Oh, dear," Ellen Lash was chattering. "Please don't kill me. Here's my purse."

"Keep it," the robber snapped. "An' for Pete's sake quit snivelin'. We don't rob women. The other lady won't be bothered, neither."

"Oh, thank you!" Ellen Lash moaned. "Thank you."

She shrank back against a coach wheel, covering her face as Sid Nelson was frisked. Nelson's pockets yielded his gold watch and a money poke, which disappeared into the sack.

Then came Kelly's turn. His nerves tightened suddenly, for it seemed to him that the bloodshot eyes of the man who had been giving the orders were studying him with unusual keenness. One of the two men, who had remained mounted, slid from his horse and came to help them search him. They found his money poke. The leader seized it eagerly, and started to dump the contents in a sack. Then he swore explosively as he saw the brass and copper contents.

"What the hell?" the man demanded, wheeling on Kelly. "Nothin' but junk. Where's your money?"

"I'm a little short," Kelly said. "I just like to collect junk. It's a hobby."

"Keep lookin'," the man said to his pals.

They went over Kelly from head to foot, turning every pocket inside out. Then they began slapping his coat and the legs of his trousers, seeking concealed money.

Suddenly Kelly understood. He had been their real quarry from the start. The other men had been searched only in a perfunctory way. But there was nothing perfunctory about the way they were going over him. They were after that $30,000, Kelly realized. Or at least seeking some evidence of its whereabouts.

He did not make the mistake of looking at Ellen Lash. He didn't need to, for he had learned enough about that young lady to guess that she wasn't missing anything and that she was capable of drawing her own conclusions.

The two men finally gave up. "Try the baggage," the leader said, and a different, harder quality had entered his voice.

The boots were opened. Carpetbags, satchels, and bags were dumped into the trail, along with a few express items and a dozen bags of mail.

Kelly, with his nerves gradually beginning to tighten up to the thrumming point, watched them fumble through the litter. Then the one who had been directing the hold-up singled out Kelly's initials on a travel-worn leather gripsack. The leader personally carried the bag off, back of a boulder, where he could not be seen. Kelly heard him dump out the contents that consisted of spare shirts and socks and a few personal papers.

The man presently came back, casting aside a fluttering handful of letters and documents that Kelly had considered worth packing in his gripsack. The man had found nothing, and his voice warned of a cold and mounting anger.

He jammed his six-shooter into Kelly's ribs. "March, you," he snarled. "The rest o' you people climb back into the coach."

Robbie spoke up. "What are you keeping Mister Brackett here for? He. . . ."

The man pushed Robbie toward the stage. "Do what I say, sister!" he exploded. "Git into that stage an' sit tight."

Robbie was white-faced. She looked like she might do a fainting act that would be the real thing, although she was not the fainting type. She also knew now what was back of Kelly's selection as the prime object for their search.

39

Kelly said: "Get into the coach, Robbie."

She hesitated, then shakily obeyed, looking fearfully at him. The others began scrambling in hastily. Ellen Lash didn't need assistance. She seemed to have forgotten her dependence on Sid Nelson. She looked at Kelly, too, and again he felt that she was measuring him as though calculating his capacity for punishment. Then she slowly entered the stage, as though in doubt about the wisdom of her obedience.

Again Kelly felt a sardonic satisfaction at seeing this second breach in her self-assurance. She looked actually worried, and at a loss.

He didn't have much time to enjoy his moment. The gun prodded him again, and its touch was not gentle. He was marched a short distance through the twilight around a curve in the trail, out of sight of the stage.

"All right," the leader said. "This is far enough. Strip, Brackett. Strip!"

Kelly said: "I haven't got it with me, mister. You're barking up the wrong tree."

A fist hit him on the jaw, knocking him to his knees. It was one of the two men who had not said a word who had swung that sneak punch.

"So you know what we're after?" the leader said. "I figured you'd guessed it now. That means you've got it, or know where it is. Peel him, boys, and go over his clothes. Or would you want to save us the trouble by talkin', Brackett?"

Kelly didn't say anything. They stripped him naked, even pulling off his boots. He stood there, shivering in the cold, watching without expression as the leader produced a knife and proceeded to rip his fine coat apart. The man fingered through every shred of lining in the hope of finding some hidden paper.

"If it's a bank draft, it won't take much space, an' might

even be sewed into his hat," he said. "Make sure. Don't overlook his boots. Cut 'em apart."

His hat, even his shoes were destroyed. The cold anger grew in the outlaws as their efforts proved futile.

"Where is it?" the leader finally asked Kelly tersely. "You might as well sing. We'll drag it out o' you, one way or another. Is it hid on that stage?"

Kelly said: "If you're through with my clothes, the pants will still keep me a little decent anyway."

He pulled on the breeches, which had suffered the least damage. One of the men slapped him so hard Kelly went down again. "How much is Luther Pritchard paying you boys for this job?" he said mildly as he got to his knees.

"Where's that money?"

Kelly came to his feet suddenly, his fist coming from his knees. It landed just below the eyes on the mask of the man who had slapped him. He felt a fierce joy as the shock of it ran through his arm. He had aimed at the point of the jaw, and found it.

The masked man backpedaled one staggering step, then hit the ground on his shoulder blades with a jolt that drove a grunt from him.

Kelly took his lumps for that. The other two were on him, kicking and beating him with fists and gun muzzles, before he could recover enough even to offer a defense. He went down, protected more by the fury of their own efforts than anything he could do.

"Don't kill him," the leader finally panted. "Hold him down."

The man Kelly had punched was back on his feet now. Two of them pinned Kelly to the ground. "Bull-headed, ain't you?" the leader said. "Now, we'll find out just how tough you really are."

With a chill Kelly saw that the man had a block of sulphur matches in his hand. They fought down his sudden frenzied outburst, and, when they had pounded him into submission again, he saw the flare of a match.

"Where's that money?" the leader gritted, and Kelly felt the sheer agony of living flame against the calf of his leg.

He yelled instinctively. Lung power seemed the only way to beat back the maddening, ravening agony that went through him. Although he yelled, it was in fury, and he was not asking for mercy. "You better kill me," he said shakily, and the leader dropped the match and looked at him expectantly, "for I'll see how you look when you yell someday."

But he knew now that was what they would do anyway when they had their way with him. Again he watched a match flare. His muscles cracked with the strain as he tried to fight them off and escape that new torture.

But it was no use. Again the excruciating torment racked him. He cursed them now, his voice shaking, and there was bloody froth on his lips where his teeth had bitten down on a lip.

Then he heard hurrying footsteps, and vaguely heard a voice say: "This girl says she's got it. She caved in when she heard Brackett yellin'."

Kelly saw the fourth masked man who had been guarding the stage passengers. With him was Ellen Lash. It was so dark, now, that her face was only an ashen blur in his swimming eyes.

She was saying, her voice thick, shaking, and she looked like she was about ready to collapse: "I've got what you've been looking for. Let him alone. For God's sake, let him alone."

"Where is it, sister?" the leader demanded.

"In my corset. Sewed up between the stays. If you'll give me. . . ."

The leader grabbed her. "I'll see for myself," he said. "I'll. . . ."

As he spoke, the masked man who had arrived with Ellen Lash was hit by something that rocked him back on his heels. Kelly heard the *crack* of a rifle and the *spat* of the bullet tearing through flesh in unison with the way the man's body jerked.

For the next few seconds, things happened in a blur he had difficulty remembering afterward. He saw the outlaw leader release Ellen Lash, and whirl, crouching. All of them were yelling, startled.

One of the two, who had been holding Kelly down, started to jump to his feet. A bullet hit him, sending him down, and he lay there an instant, shocked into rigidity while Kelly saw the first spurt of blood begin to squirt from a hole just below his elbow.

Then pistols were thundering. The two remaining masked men were shooting — but they were backing away as they shot into the twilight.

Kelly saw Ellen Lash standing there, frozen. He managed to get to his knees and dive at her, upsetting her so that she sprawled on the ground. But that sheltered her from the bullets that were crossing and re-crossing above them.

The masked man with the bullet-broken arm arose and went at a shambling, dazed run, following his two pals who were now racing for cover in the brush.

Kelly sensed what was coming and he threw himself flat again as the leader turned and emptied his last two chambers directly at him. One slug threw dirt in his face, and the other must have gone high.

The man had wanted to silence Kelly for keeps, but his gun was empty. Now he was gone, covered by brush and the gathering darkness. Kelly could hear all three of them shuttling through the brush. Presently the far sound of galloping hoofs came back, and he knew they had reached the saddle and were on their way out of the trap that had closed on them.

Ellen Lash was sitting up now, staring in the direction of a boulder from which the rescuing gunfire had come. The dead outlaw lay crumpled like a heap of rags, a yard from where Kelly lay. Kelly began to lift his head, unable to believe that it was over.

V

"HELP"

A dark-clad figure came cautiously out of the gloom, and a man's strong voice said: "Brackett? Are you hit?"

"Hello, Lee," Kelly said after a couple of tries. "This is what I call a very happy meeting. I'm in fair shape. At least there are no bullets in me, as far as I know." Kelly tried to get to his feet, then remembered his appearance. "You better look somewhere else," he mumbled to Ellen Lash. "I'm not dressed for mixed company."

She said: "I'm not looking." Then to Galvin: "Who are you?"

"Lee Galvin," he said. "I just happened along."

Galvin helped Kelly to a boulder and gave him his saddle jacket.

"I'll bring water," Ellen Lash said. "You're covered with blood, Mister Brackett." Then she went hurrying toward the nearby stream.

"I can't believe this," Kelly mumbled. "How did you happen to be here, Lee?"

44

Lee Galvin didn't answer for a moment. He bent over the dead outlaw, stripped away the mask, and struck a match to look at the staring face.

"I spotted four of Luther Pritchard's toughs pulling out of Salt Lake shortly after Robbie took the morning stage to meet you," he said. "I've been keeping an eye on one of 'em in particular. His name is Dunk Tipton." He toed the dead man impersonally. "This isn't Tipton." He shrugged. "I notched on the one I believed was Tipton, but this one stepped in line just as I cut loose. I only wanted to wing Tipton. Next to Mike Hatch, Tipton is Pritchard's top fighting man. Tipton prefers a gun. Hatch liked fists and hobnails."

"My lucky day," Kelly said.

"I figured they might be out to cause Robbie some trouble. But they only rode this far, then hung up under cover where they could watch the stage trail. I couldn't get near enough to see what they were doing. When the stage showed up, they came out fast, and were masked. It took time for me to work in close so I could see who I was shooting at. Sorry I was a little late."

Lee Galvin was reloading his cap-and-ball pistol as he offered that explanation, using a fresh chamber, already primed, which he fished from his coat pocket. He was a six-footer, with a handsome, hawk-nosed face, and striking dark eyes set beneath a high forehead. Restless, high-strung, and a few years older than Kelly, he had been everywhere in the West, seen everything before taking a job as wagon boss with Brackett & Company, when Barbas Brackett began moving logging men west into the Rubies.

Barbas Brackett had hired Lee Galvin to keep order among the lusty, brawling loggers who needed an iron hand to keep them in line. Galvin was a fighting man. He had been look-out in a big gambling house in San Francisco at one time

45

in his past and, later on, had helped establish the Butterfield stage route through the Apache country.

The loggers knew Galvin by reputation and walked easy when in his presence. But even he hadn't been able to hold them on the job when their pay stopped.

"Did Robbie meet you?" Galvin asked.

Kelly nodded. "She's on the stage. And here comes the stage back to pick us up."

The driver had got the vehicle turned around. Robbie alighted with the passengers, and, when she identified Lee Galvin, she suddenly sat on a boulder and began to weep.

Galvin started toward her, then he stopped, and Kelly knew that he had remembered that Robbie was wearing another man's ring.

Ellen Lash appeared. She had filled her poke bonnet with water, and the hat was ruined. It still held enough water to wash the blood from Kelly's face and cleanse the burned skin on his leg. She had the driver bring up her trunk, and she opened it, producing a jar of cooling cream and ointment that she applied to his injuries, and bandages.

Kelly had a moused eye and a couple of gashes on his jaw, but, as Ellen Lash worked on him, he kept watching Galvin, who stood within reach of Robbie, but not touching or speaking to her.

Robbie had quit crying. Now she said thankfully: "They didn't get what they were after, at least."

Ellen Lash finished with Kelly. She arose and walked away. Kelly gathered up enough of his scattered clothes to array himself properly. He found even his spare boots. Then he began collecting the personal papers the outlaws had scattered in their search. The majority were letters Robbie had written him in the past, but there were a few documents of value to him. There was one letter in particular that he wanted. Ellen Lash was helping him gather up the papers, but he could not find the one he was looking for. He gave it up finally, for it was dark now, deciding the wind had blown it away.

The baggage had been loaded back into the boots. The body of the dead man was wrapped in a tarp and lashed down on the deck. The passengers were climbing back into the coach.

"Was it worth the price?" Ellen Lash suddenly asked Kelly as they moved toward the coach.

"I don't know yet," Kelly said. "What is your price going to be?"

"I want to tell that to Barbas Brackett in person," she said swiftly, and climbed into the coach.

Peter Shanley eyed Kelly curiously. " 'Tis a beatin' you took, lad," he said, his attitude more friendly. "An' they even tortured you. Why was that?"

"They had the wrong person," Kelly said. "It was a clear case of mistaken identity."

"May they roast," the Irishman thundered.

"I'd prefer a little more immediate action," Kelly said grimly.

The stage rolled ahead again. Galvin had brought up his saddle horse and rode as an outrider, but it was evident he did not relish his rôle, at least when Kelly could be in the stage with Robbie.

Kelly had taken about enough for one day. He tried to ease the jolts. His seared leg was only another painful area on his body, for he had taken quite a beating from the masked men. He made a far different picture, he realized, now that his fine garb was gone. His hat was lost, and his thick dark hair was a tangled mat.

Robbie sat beside him, and he found solace in her nearness. He was glad the darkness protected him from Ellen Lash's glance. He had been stripped of his fine feathers, and even in the matter of his weighted money poke he stood exposed as a four-flusher. If Ellen Lash had been under any illusions as to the true plight of Brackett & Company, she must be fully aware of the situation now. It gave her a firmer grip on the whip-hand she held. He toughed it out, keeping his hand on the hilt of the six-shooter that he had taken from the fallen man's body to replace his own stolen gun.

There was no question in his mind but that the hold-up men had worked in secret co-operation with the same person aboard this stage who had tried to get him out of the way twice previously. Thinking back, Kelly believed that the four masked men had not been sure as to which of the passengers was Kelly Brackett when they first began operations. He guessed that he had been pointed out to them by a glance or some furtive gesture by one of the passengers.

He studied them again, wondering if the Mormon bishop was all that he pretended to be. And then there was the Irishman, who had mentioned that the money stolen from him was pay earned in Brackett employ. If Peter Shanley had been working in the Rubies, what mission had taken him to Denver, and why was he now going back on this westbound stage? Then there was the fishy-eyed, loud-talking Sid Nelson, and the gambler and the buttery-mouthed deserter. These latter two, like the bishop, were notable because of their silence. None of the three had said much about themselves.

The lights of Salt Lake City drew steadily nearer. Mountain Dell was passed, and Kelly at last began to understand that he was going to make it — alive. Luck and Lee Galvin had brought him through.

He looked at Robbie. "What time is it?"

"It can't be more than eight o'clock," she estimated.

"That," Kelly remarked for the benefit of Ellen Lash, "will give us enough leeway to take care of details before midnight."

The stage entered Salt Lake. It whirled down the wide reaches of Temple Street, passed the offices of Overland Telegraph, and the eastward line, and went on to the express office. Adjoining the express building stood the imposing, two-story, galleried Overland Hotel.

The driver bawled the announcement of the hold-up, and that soon drew a crowd. A marshal arrived, and for a quarter of an hour all the passengers answered questions.

Impatient and knowing that to tell the whole story would lead to further delay, Kelly merely told the bare facts about his ordeal, and let the marshal draw his own conclusions as to the motives. Galvin followed that cue and stated he had merely happened to come upon the hold-up by chance.

The marshal was not too keen about delving below the surface, and Kelly surmised that he suspected what was back of the reticence of the participants, but preferred to let it ride that way.

During the formalities, Robbie nudged Kelly. "Luther Pritchard," she murmured. "He's been in town a week, roosting like an old buzzard, waiting for something to die. Now he's got it, but not the way he expected." She indicated a man who stood among the throng of onlookers on the hotel gallery nearby. It was the first time Kelly had seen Pritchard in the flesh. He stared curiously.

Luther Pritchard was a solid-shouldered man of about fifty, with a big head and a mane of coarse gray hair. His mouth was small and nearly lost in the deep grooves of his wide fleshy jowls. A prominent, arched nose divided deep-set eyes that looked like little gray buttons, set in a faded cushion.

The marshal closed his investigation and told Galvin to stay in touch with him. Kelly turned to Ellen Lash. "We'll find Barbas Brackett and get down to business."

"First I'd like to take a room, where I can freshen up a little," she said. She smiled a little. "Or do I have to mention that I can't produce that money in front of gentlemen without some preliminary operations?"

"Oh, the corset," Kelly said. "Then you've really got the money."

"Of course."

Along with Robbie and Galvin, they moved to the hotel steps. Reaching the top, Kelly found himself confronted by a hulking big man, bareheaded, with a tangled shock of rusty hair gleaming in the lamplight. He had a flat, broken nose, and he showed square, tobacco-yellowed teeth in a mocking grin.

"So you came back, Brackett?" Mike Hatch said. "Do we settle it now?"

Hatch was so broad he didn't look tall. As a matter of fact, even with his sloping shoulders and long arms, that gave him a forward stoop, he topped Kelly by an inch. Half of his right ear was missing, and his left cheek was a mass of puckered scar tissue — a relic left by the calk marks of a boot in the past.

Stories — fearful stories — were told of how Mike Hatch had gouged out the eyes of opponents, bitten off ears and noses, and kicked helpless men to death. He was a fighting machine, and mercy had been left out of his make-up.

"You're too anxious to earn your money, Hatch," Kelly said.

Galvin pushed forward. "Here's one man you can't back down, Hatch," he blazed. "Let's go."

50

Kelly got between them. "And it won't be that way either, Hatch," he said. "Stay out of this, Lee."

Robbie came in then, and linked arms with Galvin. "Please!" she entreated.

Galvin heeded her, but he gave Kelly a flat look. "This is no country for you, Kelly," he said. "Better get out of it."

"I'll see to that," Mike Hatch said, and grinned. "He'll git out or crawl."

Kelly was looking at Robbie. But she swung around, presenting her back to him. She walked into the hotel sitting room with Galvin, her back rigid, her cheeks white with humiliation.

Ellen Lash's face showed nothing as she preceded Kelly through the door.

Luther Pritchard was sitting nearby in an armchair, his fine boots on the gallery rail, a cigar in his teeth.

Kelly paused, and motioned toward where the blanket-wrapped body of the dead man was being carried down the street in charge of the marshal. "The funeral expenses are on you, Pritchard," he said. Then he went on into the hotel.

VI

"LICKED AGAIN"

Ellen Lash registered under her own name. "Guard her room," Kelly requested Galvin. "And if you've got any money on you, I could use a little. The dining room is still open and I'm empty to my heels."

Galvin handed over a few gold pieces. The flat scorn was

still in his face. "Somebody's got to take care of Mike Hatch, you know," he said.

"That's one way of looking at it," Kelly replied.

"It's the only way."

"It's Pritchard's way," Kelly said. "Fighting Hatch would be playing Pritchard's game. He put Barbas Brackett out of action by that stunt. They'd still be cutting timber if Barbas was on his feet. I'm out to beat Pritchard . . . not Hatch."

He looked at Robbie for support. "That," she said with an effort, "is the sensible way of looking at it."

"Sensible," Galvin jeered, the rage tearing visibly at him. "Hell, don't you realize, Kelly, that two-thirds of your father's loggers are here, in Salt Lake, living on free lunch and free booze that Mike Hatch is setting up for them in the hangouts? Pritchard's money is paying for it. You know loggers. They won't work for a man they can't respect. They're like children. If Barbas Brackett was on his feet, they'd likely listen to him. At least he had the guts to fight it out with Hatch. But right now there's nobody. . . ." Galvin ended it with a helpless gesture.

Kelly said: "Maybe money will talk. We'll give them their back pay tonight."

"That's the easiest way out," Galvin snapped, "if it works. But maybe it won't work." He turned on his heel and climbed the stairs in the wake of Ellen Lash who a clerk was leading to a room above.

Robbie's eyes followed him. She scrubbed her kerchief nervously in her hands, and Kelly knew that she had nothing to say to him.

"I'll go and tell Barbas you're here," she said, breaking the awkward silence between them. And she hurried out.

Kelly went into the dining room alone. In spite of his wolf hunger the food tasted like gall.

52

Ellen Lash presently reappeared, with Galvin hovering over her like a grim-eyed guardian spirit. She had changed to a dark, bustled dress and a short, puffed-sleeved jacket. She had hung her hair in a snood, in lieu of a hat. She was tightly stayed, to bring out the slim-waisted fashion of the day, and didn't look like she had just undergone a wearisome trip by stage. She was dressed for the kill, Kelly reflected, her spirits buoyed by the anticipation of her vengeance.

Kelly joined them and they left the hotel and headed for the residence that Barbas Brackett used as his office and living quarters. It stood not far from his wagon yards, and their route took them through the rougher section of the town.

"You have the money?" Kelly asked.

"Yes, Mister Brackett."

"In cash?" Kelly asked curiously. "Paper money?"

"Thirty federal gold notes of one thousand dollars denomination. That was the only kind of money that could be sewed into a person's corset."

Kelly eyed her trim figure. "I'd never have believed you were so well padded," he drawled. "Your shape doesn't seem to have changed."

She said lightly: "You flatter me. Fortunately I had the foresight to bring along replacements so that I could retain my silhouette. My original stays are now damaged beyond repair, but I am well armored, nevertheless."

"Gold notes are acceptable here?" Kelly questioned.

She nodded. "Brigham Young's bank will give you hard yellow money for them without question. He is loyal to the Union. I made sure of that before I started."

"You are a very practical person," Kelly commented. "You haven't overlooked a bet, have you?"

"That," she said, "remains to be seen."

Robbie was waiting at the door for them. She admitted them to a severely furnished room. Beneath the glow of a shaded oil lamp Barbas Brackett sat in a wheelchair, with his splinted leg propped on a bench. Crutches stood near at hand. His powerful, hard-boned face bore the purple marks of scars that were nearly healed, but his eyes, fierce and proud, had lost none of their harsh impact.

He sat there looking at Kelly, and, although this was the first time they had really met face to face in five years, he only grunted an acknowledgment. Barbas Brackett had been unconscious that day two months in the past when Kelly had arrived in the logging camp just as the fight with Mike Hatch had ended.

There was no forgiveness in Barbas Brackett. Kelly's mother had died when he was seven, and Barbas had aspired to rear his son in his own ruthless, two-fisted image. He had seen to it that Kelly had boxing lessons along with his schooling. As a boy, Kelly had found himself tossed like a pit bull into fights with tough street gamins. That was his father's way of giving him practical experience.

It brought the inevitable reaction. Growing to manhood, Kelly, in sheer rebellion, became a spendthrift and a fashion plate, preferring the company of gay young blades and flashy women. After an episode that brought his expulsion from college, his father disowned him, denouncing him as a weakling and a wastrel. As though freed of a burden, Kelly had steadied. He had gone into the Minnesota logging country, and had been there five years when his father signed the Overland Telegraph contract.

He had kept in close touch with Robbie all that time. She knew that he was camp boss of one of the big companies in the north woods. She had come to him personally when his father was moving his first crews West. Robbie was going to the new job, too, as soon as she closed up the affairs of the St. Louis office.

"Barbas has his hands full this time," she had told Kelly frankly. "He's older than he realizes and he needs a timber boss he can trust. He needs you."

"Did he send you to me?" Kelly had asked.

Robbie had looked at him frankly. "No, Kelly. I'm the one that's asking you to come."

Kelly had been waiting a long time to hear something like that from Robbie. He had kissed her, and she had responded. That was the day he had slipped his ring on her finger.

So he had headed West a month later to join her and make peace with his father. But, during that interval, the crisis had come in the affairs of Brackett & Company. Kelly had reached the logging camp in the Rubies just as his father was being carried away from that bloody fight with Mike Hatch.

Hatch, learning that another Brackett was on hand, had started hunting Kelly with the intention of working him over. But Kelly had taken the next stage East, refusing to meet his challenger. He had gone back to St. Louis, to beg or borrow the money needed to fend off Luther Pritchard.

Now his father was treating him with bare tolerance. "So they put a little heat on you this evenin'," Barbas Brackett said with sour humor. "Robbie tells me some of Luther Pritchard's huskies got rough with you."

"A little," Kelly said.

"I bet you yelled."

"I yelled," Kelly nodded. "Plenty."

"Gave head like a bull calf at weanin' time, huh?"

"That's right," Kelly agreed.

Barbas Brackett said: "Bah." His sultry glance swung belligerently to Ellen Lash, who had remained in the background, out of direct reach of the lamplight. "Who's this?" he demanded. "Where's the money Robbie said you was bringin' with you?"

Kelly eyed Robbie questioningly. She shrugged, and he understood that she hadn't told his father the full story.

"This," Kelly said, "is Ellen Lash. She's got thirty thousand dollars with her. She's ready to talk business."

"Lash! Ellen Lash!" Barbas Brackett's voice was like metal. Ellen Lash walked into the light. Brackett's big frame pulled straight in the wheelchair, and he sat there motionless, staring with the grimness of a strong man suddenly aware of his helpless position.

"You're Kendall Lash's daughter," he said slowly. "You look like your mother did twenty-five years ago."

"So I've been told," she answered levelly. "But I also resemble my father in many ways."

Barbas Brackett was silent a moment, staring at her. But Kelly knew he wasn't seeing her. He was seeing things in the past, twenty-five years in the past. Finally he spoke harshly. "What do you want here, Miss Lash?"

"I have the money," Ellen Lash said. She produced a thick roll of bills, and placed it on a table.

Barbas Brackett turned furiously on Kelly. "You know better'n this," he said hoarsely.

"There was nobody else who would loan money to a busted company," Kelly interrupted him. "It's your last chance . . . your only chance."

Barbas Brackett's big hands clamped hard on the arms of his chair. "I might have known you'd bungle it," he said bitterly. He glared at the girl. "Well, let's hear it! What interest do you want for a ninety-day demand? I'm in the habit of payin' eight percent."

"No interest," Ellen Lash said. "My terms are simple.

This is an investment with me. All I ask is fifty-one percent ownership of Brackett and Company."

Robbie spoke angrily. "Why, that's absurd."

"Is it?" Ellen Lash asked quietly.

Barbas Brackett stared at her queerly. The fury had burned out inside him. "It took twenty-five years, didn't it?" he said with musing irony. "An' now one of the Lashes is gettin' square with me . . . for everything."

"Not everything," Ellen Lash said. "This is only the first installment on the debt."

"Surely, Barbas, you don't intend to give in to any such terms?" Robbie exploded. "Why, that would give this . . . this girl control of the company. Your company. She could over-rule even you."

Barbas Brackett glanced significantly at a banjo clock that was ticking on the wall. "Got any other means of raising that much money in less'n two hours, Robbie?" he asked sourly.

Robbie had no answer for that. Barbas Brackett turned on Kelly. "I figured you had some brains, even if they forgot to put any sand in your backbone. Or maybe you're getting something out of this?"

"Sure," Kelly said stonily. "I got something out of it. A crack on the head from a blackjack, live matches on my skin, and the whisper of a bullet that was meant for my gizzard. That's what I got out of it, Barbas. But, of course, you won't believe that."

Barbas Brackett's gaunt face did not soften. He only said to Robbie: "Draw up the papers. Lee, you go fetch Luther Pritchard. Tell him to bring his damned promissory note with him. It'll be almost worth the price to see his face when I burn that note."

"I've already had the terms of partnership drawn up,"

Ellen Lash said, drawing some papers from the bosom of her dress. "They are short and to the point, and plainly worded, but you can call in a lawyer to look them over if you wish."

"You came loaded for bear, didn't you?" Kelly commented.

"For wolves is the proper way of putting it."

Barbas read the papers slowly, carefully. "All right," he said. "It's plain enough. Give me a pen."

"I insist . . . ," Robbie began.

"There's no other way," Barbas snapped. "She's got me. Why wriggle? She only enjoys it that much more." Grimly he scratched his name on the two articles of partnership. He tossed one to Ellen Lash and let the other remain on the table. There was a bitter, mirthless smile on his unshaven face. "Licked again," he commented. "First, I let a jellyfish like Pritchard run me into a hole. Then Mike Hatch took me to a cleanin', an' now a damned little schemin' petticoat has taken my company away from me."

VII

"ORDERS"

Luther Pritchard arrived presently. He came alone. He was suave, but a wariness showed in his manner.

When he saw the money on the table, Kelly noticed that the man permitted himself only the merest flicker of an expression of chagrin.

Barbas Brackett slapped $25,000 in front of him. "Count it, Pritchard," he said. "Then hand over that damned note. I'm going to use it to light my cigar."

Pritchard's opaque glance flitted around the group and settled questioningly on Ellen Lash.

Kelly said: "Your toughs almost got it, Pritchard. Next time, tell 'em to search the ladies first."

"You talk in riddles, my friend," Pritchard remarked blandly. "I have no idea as to what you're driving at. In fact, I'm not even interested. Good evening." He handed over his promissory note, picked up the money, and walked out, unruffled.

Barbas Brackett stared after him, disappointed. "Pritchard took his lickin' like a dog," he commented.

"He isn't licked yet," Kelly said. "This is only the end of the first round."

"The hell he ain't. He's got no toehold on me now."

"Pritchard is out for bigger game than just Brackett and Company," Kelly declared. He was looking at Ellen Lash now. "As you know, Overland Telegraph was guaranteed a big bonus and an annual subsidy by the government if it completed its line before winter. That offer lapses if they fail."

"What's that got to do with it?" Barbas challenged impatiently. "They can finish it next spring if. . . ."

"Luther Pritchard swings plenty of weight in Washington," Kelly interrupted. "He's all ready to start building his own telegraph lines through from California in the spring, under a new agreement with the government. It'll leave Overland out in the cold. Overland couldn't compete with a government-subsidized line."

"Where'd you hear this?" Barbas growled.

"In Saint Louis. Bill North of Pioneer Bank told me."

"If Bill North said it, then it's true," Barbas admitted. "He's got his finger on every political deal in the country."

Kelly eyed Ellen Lash. "How do you feel about your bargain now? We've still got to get those logs out before snow flies, and it may snow soon in the Rubies."

She smiled a little ruefully. "I must admit that I might have thought a second time if I'd known this." She shrugged. "But you have my money. I don't imagine you would get it back for me, even if Luther Pritchard would consent."

"He'd be only too blasted glad to kick back," Barbas snapped. "But I wouldn't."

"It seems I'll have to hope that nothing interferes with the logging before the camp is snowed in," she remarked. "I imagine, under the circumstances, that Luther Pritchard will wish just the opposite."

"You guessed it." Kelly nodded. "That's why I said this was only the end of the first round. From now on something tells me the going gets tougher."

She was putting on her gloves. "I know it will be distasteful," she said, "but I'm not familiar with this town, and it is rather late for an unescorted lady on the street. If one of you gentlemen would be so good as to see me to my hotel. . . ."

"You brought her here, Kelly," Barbas Brackett said uncompromisingly. "You can take her away. Lose her somewhere, for all I care."

Kelly looked ruefully at Robbie. He had counted on having a long talk with her. There was a lot he had to say. Then he noticed that Robbie was no longer wearing his ring. That hit him hard. Drearily he realized that Robbie might listen to him with her ears, but not with her heart. She had withdrawn that far from him since he had refused for the second time to fight Mike Hatch. She did not move or speak. She only stood there. In her face he saw that same remoteness and lack of a common ground that he had found in Lee Galvin and had always found in his father. So he offered his arm to Ellen Lash.

They walked out into the crisp, thin darkness of the Utah night. The scent of wild sage came in from the land, mingling with the homely presence of tamed fields. The leaves of trees the Mormons had transplanted from other lands were dead and crackling underfoot, and the mountain streams the Saints had diverted down each street in small gutter channels made a clean and soothing refrain. The Mormon city had gone to bed at its usual sedate hour, but there were lights and conviviality in that section where the non-believers gathered.

The girl walked in silence. They passed a noisy, canvas-built hang-out whose lamp-lit sign proclaimed it as the Trail's End. Glancing through the door, Kelly saw that the place was crowded with whiskery, red-shirted men. He knew they were freighters and loggers from the Brackett camps, for he saw Mike Hatch standing at the bar, and it was evident that he was the cock of the walk there.

Kelly, in spite of himself, favored his singed leg a trifle. "At the hotel," Ellen Lash said, "I'll take a look at your leg again. And that eye needs attention."

"Why this sudden consideration for the health of one of the Bracketts?" Kelly said wearily. "Up to now you've been hitting me with everything you could lay hands on . . . including white feathers."

"It's purely a business proposition with me, Mister Brackett. I don't want to lose the only man who really knows how to log a country, now that Barbas Brackett is laid up."

"You seem to know a lot about Brackett and Company," Kelly said, nettled.

"Yes, thanks to Peter Shanley."

"Shanley? So that's how it is?"

"Peter Shanley used to be with my father years ago," she said. "I knew he had been working as a crew boss on this Brackett job in the Rubies. So I sent word by pony and wire for him to meet me at Denver. That was when I had made up my mind to loan you the money. He told me all the facts that I didn't know already. But there wasn't much I hadn't learned beforehand in Saint Louis."

"Except about Pritchard," Kelly reminded her.

"That's one detail that escaped me," she acknowledged.

"You're so damned bright, you ought to get along in the world," Kelly said sullenly. "Well, at least this seems to clear Shanley of trying to shoot and blackjack me. I wonder if it could have been that young, baby-faced lout who. . . ."

"It wasn't. Not that jellyfish. He had nothing to do with it."

Kelly twisted around, staring at her intently. "Are you trying to say that you know which one of those stage passengers was back of all the misery that was dealt to me?" he demanded.

"And what would you do if I told you?"

Kelly didn't know that his fingers had closed fiercely on her arm until he saw her lips part in an involuntary grimace of pain. But she didn't utter any audible sound of protest.

"And what do you think I'll do?" he asked, and there was something wild and heedless welling up in him. "Have you ever been held down while a man touched a lighted match to you to make you yell? Who was it? Was it that Mormon bishop?"

"There's been enough trouble for one day," she said, drawing away from him. "And . . . and enough killing. Those men aren't important. No more important than Mike Hatch, really. If you can ignore Hatch, then you let this other thing ride, too."

"So I'm ignoring Hatch? That's a nice way of putting it. Thanks. Other folks have different explanations. I didn't expect that from you."

62

She said coolly: "It would be insane to fight him tonight, the shape you're in. Don't let that hot-headed Galvin, or your father, or that girl you're in love with, drive you from your purpose. You can't get logs out of the mountains if you're in the hospital, or in your grave."

"Who said I was intending to fight Hatch tonight or any other night?" Kelly snapped.

"You're not hard to read. You've decided to go back to that honky-tonk we just passed, and fight it out with Hatch. You made up your mind to look him up when you noticed that Miss McDowell had taken off your ring."

"You see too much for your own good," Kelly said weakly.

"She merely removed the ring for safekeeping when the stage was held up," Ellen Lash said. "You shouldn't jump to the wrong conclusions . . . or give up that easy."

"Who said I'd given up?" Kelly exploded.

"We were talking about Mike Hatch," she countered. "Let's stick to the point. They've driven you to it, your sweetheart and your father and Galvin. It's against your better judgment, but you're weak enough to try to prove your manhood, even though you believe you'll get licked. That is exactly what Luther Pritchard wants. It'll have the company without a man competent enough to finish that job in the Rubies. Lee Galvin can't. He hasn't had experience in a big timber camp. Your father can't. He's an invalid." She paused, letting him think it over. "I'm looking at it from a mercenary standpoint," she added. "I've got more money involved in this than I want to lose. And by the way, could you advance me a little cash?"

"Cash? How much?"

"Well, enough to buy breakfast at least." She was in earnest in spite of her smile. She said lightly: "I had to scrape the bottom of the barrel to raise thirty thousand dollars. I sold everything, even my spare clothing and what few pieces of jewelry I had. I had just enough left to buy my stage fare west."

"So that's why . . . ?"

"That's why I was forced to smile for my dinner all the way from Atchison," she admitted. "It was that or starvation. And I do just love to eat regularly. It's one luxury I would abandon only with the greatest reluctance."

Kelly laughed ruefully. "And I thought I was the one who was putting up a real bluff with my fine clothes and salted money poke. Two of us, traveling on our nerve, but I was the one that went hungry." He handed her the money that remained from what Lee Galvin had loaned him. "I'll raise more tomorrow," he said.

"I'll pay it back," she promised, and her primness had suddenly returned.

They entered the hotel. The sitting room was almost deserted at this late hour. The clerk's counter was closed for the night. Peter Shanley sat drowsily in a chair, smoking a pipe, ignoring them so pointedly that Kelly knew he had been waiting there for Ellen Lash's return. Peter Shanley had appointed himself her protector. There were only two other men in the room. They were in a far corner, playing euchre. A whiskey bottle and glasses stood between them. One was Sid Nelson, the affable man who had been on the stage with them. His companion was a blocky, sun-cured man with bushy black hair who wore a dark slouch hat, a fringed buckskin jacket, and had his dark breeches stuffed into spurred boots.

Sid Nelson, his back to the door, had just put his hand in his coat pocket and drawn something forth at which he glanced hastily. He was yawning, and that was a part of the natural gesture of a man who was looking at his watch to learn the time.

64

Kelly took a few more steps, when the significance of that it him like a slap in the face. He paused in mid-stride.

"No," Ellen Lash breathed in his ear, her voice suddenly anicky. "Not here. Don't. . . ."

"That watch," he murmured. "I saw 'em take it from Nelson today and drop it in their gunny sack. Now he's got it ack. He's got it in his pocket where it can't be seen. But he orgot, and looked at the time."

She couldn't evade his insistent eyes. She nodded slightly. I began to suspect it after you were blackjacked at Bridger," he whispered. "Nelson was the only one whose whereabouts I ouldn't account for when that happened. But I wasn't sure ntil I pretended to faint into his arms when the stage was held p. That's why I swore at you when you lifted me out of the tage. I felt the blackjack under his coat. He carries it slung bove his elbow. And I felt a Derringer in one sleeve, at least. 'm not sure what else he may have in the way of weapons."

"You learned enough to scare me at least," Kelly said. And something tells me his card-playing pal is the one who ut the torch to me. He probably just got back to town."

"But why . . . ?" she began to protest.

"Go to your room," Kelly said. He left her at the foot of he stairs.

VIII

"FIGHT!"

Kelly walked without haste toward the two card players. They did not look at him, but he sensed that they were aware f him. He guessed they had been waiting here, expecting him to return with Ellen Lash. They had orders, no doubt, to keep an eye on him.

He paused beside the table. "Howdy, Nelson," he said easily. "My watch is stopped. Have you the time?"

Sid Nelson's mind was not too keen. He had been expecting something else. That familiar request fooled him. Force of habit caused his hand to start involuntarily toward his pocket. Then he knew! He darted a quick, startled glance at his companion, and the affability was gone from him instantly.

Kelly looked at the bloodshot eyes of the dark-visaged men, remembering those eyes he had seen through the slits in the gunny-sack mask. He saw Sid Nelson hitch around in his chair, and knew the man was moving to shake the Derringer that the girl had mentioned into action.

Kelly instantly drove the heel of his right palm upward beneath Nelson's chin. It came within an ace of snapping the man's neck. He went over backwards, his barrel chair tilting. He flailed his arms wildly in a futile attempt to break his fall.

The dark-jowled man, impelled by his position in the chair, was trying to get his six-shooter clear, but Kelly upended the table and plunged forward with that as a battering ram. Unable to escape from the chair in time, the man overturned and Kelly and the table landed crushingly on top of him, pinning him to the floor.

Kelly jerked his own pistol. Sid Nelson had rolled free of his capsized chair and had his Derringer rising. Kelly reached out and chopped the eight-inch barrel of his heavy cap-and-ball pistol down on Nelson's arm. He put all his strength back of it, and heard the bones in Nelson's arm snap. The Derringer exploded, its reports thick and heavy against the confining walls, but the bullet went into the floor.

Then Kelly brought his gun muzzle up in a side-slash

against Nelson's face. Blood spurted, and the man's nose flattened. He toppled on his side, writhing and moaning.

Meanwhile, the other man had managed to squirm partly from beneath the table. However, he was belly down, pinned by Kelly's weight. He tried to twist around so as to bring his six-shooter to bear. Kelly rammed a foot against the back of the man's head, punching his face hard against the splintery floor. He reached out, got a grip on the pistol, and wrenched it away. Then he rolled off the table, dragged the stunned man partly to his feet. Kelly drove his fist into his quarry's face. Blood and loose teeth flew. The man sagged back against the wall, and slid to a sitting position, his eyes glassy.

Kelly lifted an oil lamp from a wall bracket, and hurled the chimney aside. He stood there with the naked, swaying flame on the wick, looking down at the man who had tortured him.

"I wonder how loud you'll yell?" he said.

As though through a bleak fog he now saw that Ellen Lash hadn't left. She was standing on the stairs, her face, white rigid with a fixed horror. Peter Shanley was standing in the background, also, with something of that same look on his Celtic face. The fog faded, and all things in the room came suddenly into focus. As quickly as it had come the black, destructive fury left Kelly.

He set the lamp down. "All right," he spoke thickly. He looked at the two dazed men. "Tell Luther Pritchard to do his own fighting. Now get out of here."

He hoisted them to their feet, and headed them toward the door. Bleeding, dazed, they went out, stumbled down the steps, heading away into the darkness.

Peter Shanley said wonderingly: "One o' them was none other than Dunk Tipton, me boy. He is a killer. 'Twould be well to watch yourself with care from now on."

Ellen Lash looked a little limp. She put a hand to her forehead and murmured: "Don't ever let yourself go like that again. You'll kill somebody."

Kelly listened to hurrying footsteps approaching the hotel. Then Robbie came racing up the steps into the room. She was excited, weeping. "Kelly! Lee Galvin is fighting Mike Hatch. You've got to stop it!"

"Where?"

"At the Trail's End," she gasped. "He went there to challenge Hatch. Hurry."

Kelly swore under his breath. He began running.

He could hear the sound of conflict before he reached the Trail's End. The sharp spat of fists and the subdued sigh of watching men came from the lamp-lit canvas walls.

The entrance was packed ten-deep with onlookers. Kelly forced his way into the front rank. A big circle had been cleared on the sawdust-covered dirt floor. There, Lee Galvin and Mike Hatch were hammering each other.

Galvin was bare to the waist, the tatters of his shirt hanging from his belt. He was bloody, and his torso had the marble pallor of exhaustion. His eyes were staring, rolling a little to show the whites.

Hatch was spattered with gore, also, and some of it was his own. He had taken punishment, but Kelly saw that Galvin was just about out on his feet. Only his pride was keeping him erect. Hatch was circling him, measuring him with wicked calm. Then Hatch swung the knock-out punch to the jaw. Galvin saw it coming, but didn't have the co-ordination to parry or duck. He stopped that punch with his jaw, and then he reeled back. Slowly he pitched forward on his face in the sawdust.

Hatch walked in, lifting a hobbed boot to cave in Galvin's face. Kelly was moving across the circle as that last punch landed. He shoved Hatch off balance, and the kick that had been aimed at the helpless man missed. Hatch sprawled to a knee.

"You've knocked him out, Hatch," Kelly said. "That's enough. No gouging. No boot-work. He's too game a man for that. This fight is over."

Hatch got up, grinning uglily as he peered at Kelly. "At least Galvin had the guts to fight," he said. "Maybe you'd like to take up where he left off. I'm ready. He just got me warmed up." Hatch turned to the circle of men. The majority of them were Brackett freighters and loggers. "Ten to one he crawls out of it again," he added. "Any takers, boys?"

They watched Kelly, awaiting his answer. Their code was primitive, simple. They lived close to the earth, from day to day, and measured a man's courage by the strength of his fists.

Kelly stood there, debating. He had fought a few tough ones in the past. He had won his share of fights, but he had been licked once or twice, too. He knew the taste of defeat, the barren savor of victory. He had never fought a man as good as Mike Hatch.

"You boys want to see me take a trimming, don't you?" he finally said. "All right. I'll make a deal with you. I'll fight big Mike . . . but only after the job in the Rubies is finished. Help me get those poles out of the mountains so Overland can finish stringing wire. Then Hatch will get his chance to show how good he really is."

"Don't fall for that," Hatch scoffed. "He's only squirmin' out of it ag'in, like I said he would."

"You men welched on an agreement with Barbas Brackett," Kelly said, ignoring Hatch. "Real loggers don't let another man down when the going gets tough."

"How about our pay?" one of them hooted. "I got more'n a month's wages comin'."

"You'll get it tonight," Kelly said.

"Tonight! Hell, we all know we'll be workin' for Luther Pritchard tomorrow. Everybody knows Barbas has lost the contract."

"Wrong," Kelly snapped. "Prichard's note was paid off tonight. Barbas Brackett is still boss of Brackett and Company."

As he said it a little shock hit Kelly as he remembered that his father was no longer the head of his company in actuality. Ellen Lash now had the controlling interest. But he let it ride, for he sensed that he had them listening to him.

"He's lyin'!" Mike Hatch bawled. "He's. . . ."

"He's tellin' the truth!" the voice of Barbas Brackett boomed.

Barbas stood in the doorway, poised indomitably on his crutches, wearing his splints like a wounded lion. He had a heavy canvas bag in his hand, and he thumped it now against a whiskey barrel so that every man heard the unmistakable *chink* of coin. "Gold from the vaults of the Mormon bank," he snapped. "Step up, men, an' draw what's comin' to you. My secretary has the payroll ready."

Robbie, with a ledger in her hand, was standing there with him. Kelly saw her looking with horror at Galvin who still lay there in the sawdust, bloody and dazed.

Barbas Brackett's fierce eyes singled out men in the crowd. "You Shamus, an' Shorty Joyce, an' Ike Salters? What kind of quitters are you that you leave a job half finished an' come to booze on the money furnished by a soft-bellied worm like Luther Pritchard?" He went on, naming men, castigating them, reminding them of past favors he had done them.

Barbas might be a willful man, but he also knew when to press a psychological advantage. He swung down the room

70

on his crutches, pushing among them. He was making full capital of his rôle as a martyr rising from the sickbed to lead a cause that had been given up as lost.

"We're startin' back to the Rubies tonight!" he thundered. "Are you tough enough to follow men like me an' Lee Galvin, or would you rather stay in Salt Lake an' fill your hides with rotgut while real men help build the biggest telegraph line in the world?" He added, without a glance at Kelly: "I'm puttin' Lee Galvin in full charge of the timber gang. But I'll be on the job, too, as much as this leg permits, an' I'll take my place on the end of a saw if it comes to that."

He turned. Like a pied piper he led them out of the Trail's End. They flowed through the door at his heels, half drunk and swayed by the sentimentality of their natures.

Hatch said grimly to Kelly: "Your round, Brackett. But they'll hold you to that brag you made about fightin' me. An' I'll hold you to it, too." Then Hatch added softly: "If you live that long."

Kelly saw that both Robbie and Ellen had entered this place, forbidden to decent women, and were working over Lee Galvin. They had brought water from the bar, and Robbie was sitting in the sawdust with Galvin's head in her lap while Ellen washed away the blood and stretched his arms to restore circulation.

Galvin was beginning to revive. Kelly bent over him, probed him for broken bones. Galvin had taken a beating, but as far as Kelly could make out, he had escaped any lasting damage. Galvin finally got up groggily. He looked up at Kelly. "So I got licked," he muttered bitterly.

It was Robbie who answered that. "You lost a fight," she corrected fiercely, "but you didn't get licked. A man is licked only when he quits." She was stroking Galvin's hair.

Kelly thought: *He's won himself a woman.* He helped up

71

Galvin and steadied him until his head cleared. They walked out of the Trail's End.

The Brackett & Company's corrals and wagon yard, a block away, were swarming with activity. Barbas Brackett was losing no time getting out freight and supply wagons to transport his truant men back to the job.

Kelly gazed bleakly in that direction. "I'll sign up at the usual pay for a logger, if you want me, Lee," he said.

Galvin stared at him. "How come?"

"Barbas has put you permanently in charge of the crew," Kelly explained.

Ellen spoke. "I will countermand that order. Mister Brackett has had experience at logging, I believe, while Mister Galvin knows more about the freighting and supply end of the job. I hope you will find that satisfactory, Mister Galvin?"

Galvin hesitated, eyeing Kelly dubiously. "She's the boss, I suppose." He shrugged. "I'll go along with the play until we see how it works out."

IX

"RUBIES"

Barbas Brackett took Ellen's change of orders in sardonic silence. Being overruled in his own company was a bitter pill to swallow.

Anxious to get to the Rubies, Kelly had a light, canvas-topped wagon hooked up for his own use, with four mules in harness. He selected a young, freckled Missourian to drive the first leg of the trip, and intended to pick up fresh teams and drivers at relay stations that his father maintained for his freight teams at fifty-mile intervals along the route to the Rubies. Busy up to the last minute he, at last, tossed a Henry rifle into the wagon, and crawled aboard, pulling out in advance of the slower-moving freight wagons in which the loggers were piling.

He was dog-tired, but Ellen and Robbie had treated his bruises again, and his foot and head were no longer as troublesome. He had rounded up a green Mackinaw, a flannel shirt, and a knitted woolen cap with a yellow tassel in the north-woods style. Logging garb gave him a sense of reality in a hectic world that was rapidly becoming more unreal to him. Crawling forward into the wagon, into which he had placed a pallet of buffalo robes, he was thinking about getting some solid rest, for he knew that he would be on the jump once he reached the Rubies.

The wagon was hitting the chuckholes in fine style as the driver let the mules warm up.

A feminine voice said: "Ouch! You're on my foot!"

It was Ellen. Kelly steadied himself in the careening wagon and cursed tiredly and sincerely. He had left her at the hotel more than two hours ago.

"A lady is present, you know," she reproved him.

"This is as far as you go!" Kelly raged. "You can't do this."

"If either of us leave, my friend, it will be you," she snapped. "I hired you, and I can fire you."

"This is a forty-eight hour trip," Kelly argued. "Nearly three hundred miles of fast travel. If you're going to the Rubies, why not travel with Miss McDowell and the others in the freight wagons. It'll be more comfortable, at least."

"I don't believe Miss McDowell cares for my company," she said, invisible in the darkness. "And I'm sure Barbas Brackett doesn't."

"But, of course, I'm delighted to have you," Kelly said witheringly.

"If it's my comfort you're worrying about, I will not complain," she said. "If it's my reputation or your own that's bothering you, think nothing of it. I have a pistol, and it's loaded. The driver knows I'm here. We're going to need all the help we can get in the mountains. I can cook, wash dishes."

"It's your funeral," Kelly said surlily. "And I'm too tired to argue. Good night, and pleasant dreams."

He began arranging a buffalo robe. She was somewhere close at hand in the darkness, for this wagon wasn't very big. She was too damned close, he discovered, for he suddenly got his hand tangled up in her hair.

She freed herself. "Remember, I have that gun right beside me," she warned primly.

Kelly said: "Oh, hell!" He rolled up in the robe and closed his eyes.

"Another thing," Ellen said presently. "Peter Shanley told me to tell you that Dunk Tipton rode out of town not long before we started. Peter Shanley kept an eye on Tipton after that trouble at the hotel. He said you ought to be careful. Tipton will try to get even for the way you manhandled him."

Kelly came wide-awake instantly. "How far ahead of us did Tipton leave?"

"It couldn't have been more than five or ten minutes. Peter found me just before you came to the wagon."

Kelly thought that over for a minute. He sat up wearily. "All right," he said. "You win. I'll play it safe. I'll do my sleeping next winter." He spoke to Bud Emerson, the young driver. "You hit the blankets for a while, Bud. I'll drive."

He took over the reins, but he didn't climb onto the seat. He stood in the wagon bed, resting his elbows on the back of the seat, and then he hit on an idea. He took off his Mackinaw, and had Bud Emerson stuff a buffalo robe into it and buckle the Mackinaw around it. Kelly placed his yellow logging cap on top of the dummy and managed to prop it fairly securely on the seat by suspending it by a lashing from the overhead wagon bow.

"You two lie flat and get some sleep," he ordered. "Nothing will likely happen anyway."

There was only the starlight, and the dummy on the seat might look enough like a man to delude anyone in ambush. Kelly remained crouched back of the seat, wielding the reins, and watching the Stygian shadows along the trail. He had the Henry rifle alongside him, and his pistol was loaded and within quick reach.

The mules were traveling at a steady, jingling gait along a level trail. Daybreak was still three hours away.

The miles passed. The dank smell of the salt-impregnated lake strengthened. After a time the trail wound through a ghostly expanse where salt and alkali lay like a sheet of snow over the flats. Even the starlight was brighter here.

Kelly fought overpowering drowsiness. He caught himself dozing off at times, and he tried the heroic method of rubbing a pinch of tobacco on an eyelid. The smarting aroused him, kept him busy, and all his miseries came crowding back upon him.

Then it came so unexpectedly it left him frozen with surprise for an instant. A gun began flashing not fifty yards ahead of the lead mule, and slightly off the trail, where a salt hummock, crowned with tenacious brush, offered a hide-out. The stuffed Mackinaw jacket jerked to the impact of two bullets, and Kelly heard the vicious scream of one past his ear.

Then he was shooting back with the Henry. The mules,

panicked by the gunfire, swerved violently off the trail, and the wagon went up on two wheels. It hung there an instant, but righted itself. Kelly sawed the mules to a stop and sensed that two more bullets had torn through the canvas top past him.

He leaped from the wagon. Against the background of alkali he knew he was a fair target, but he wanted to draw the fire on himself, away from the girl and Bud Emerson and from the team. He was moving, zigzagging as he ran. The ambusher's gun kept flaming, and Kelly heard slugs pass him, and one kicked up the alkali at his feet.

The hidden man had a Henry repeater, also, and suddenly it went silent. Kelly knew he had emptied the gun. But there was no question but that the man was armed with a pistol. And there was no doubt that Dunk Tipton was doing the shooting. Tipton was a pistol expert.

Kelly was moving. He ran toward that hummock, which proved to be some twenty yards or more across. It rose some six feet above the flat, and its weedy salt brush formed a thin tangle at its crest. Tipton was on the opposite side of the hummock. Kelly abandoned his own rifle now, knowing that the finish of this would be at close quarters. He crouched there an instant, stilling his breathing.

The mules had kept running, and he could hear the wagon wheels bouncing in the darkness, along with the pound of hoofs. But Emerson and the girl were out of range at least.

Then he could hear nothing at all. He began moving, placing one foot before another, circling the rough contour of the hummock. He paused every few strides to give his lungs a chance to settle, and to listen. All he heard was the staccato throb of his pulse in his ears. He found a loose chunk of alkali and tossed it up into the brush. It struck and rattled a moment, and then the silence came again.

But he knew Tipton was still there, stalking him, just as he was stalking Tipton. Kelly crouched a moment, and now even the far sound of hoofs and wheels had died, indicating that the mules had come to a stop.

He knew Tipton was near, for the clean night air brought the odor of tobacco and a whiskey breath. Kelly realized the man was up on the hummock itself. He rose to his height, ducked back instantly. And that saved his life, for a bullet sliced through the spot where he had exposed his head.

He rose again, spilling three shots in the direction of the gun flashes. Tipton was no more than thirty feet from him, but he heard no indication that he had scored a hit. He had three shots left in his gun, and he had not brought an extra chamber. He could not reload a cap-and-ball pistol under these conditions.

He crept slightly a few yards to his right, then arose to his feet again, ducking back. He drew no fire then. But he heard faint movement. Tipton was either retreating, or coming at him.

This had to be finished now. Kelly rose and then went charging up the hummock, through the brittle salt brush. It was a frontal attack, and Dunk Tipton, startled, opened up on him. A bullet tugged at Kelly's shirtsleeve, and he fired back into the gun flash. He fired again, and now he had only one bullet left. He went charging ahead, and Tipton stood, shooting as fast as he could roll the hammer. Kelly kept coming at him, and Tipton was trying to run away from him as he fired.

Kelly fired his last bullet, and then he stopped and felt his knees shaking. Dunk Tipton had uttered his first sound — a strangled gasp. Then Tipton went down, rolling a few yards to the bottom of the hummock.

Kelly moved cautiously to his side after a time. Then he

jammed the empty gun back in his shoulder holster. Dunk Tipton was dead. He had two bullet holes in him. One of Kelly's first shots must have got him, but Kelly knew that it was his last bullet that had finished him.

He heard the wagon approaching, and he called out. It loomed up against the alkali, and he walked to it, climbed beneath the top, and said: "All right, Bud. You can drive. I don't look for any more trouble tonight."

Neither Bud nor Ellen asked questions. Kelly rolled up in a buffalo robe. He was chilled to the bone and he was shaking. In spite of his weariness he could not sleep. He believed Ellen had gone to sleep for she had not said anything for some time.

The first light of dawn was reaching beneath the wagon top when she spoke. "I bet Lee Galvin a hundred dollars that you'd fight Mike Hatch," she murmured.

"What did you use for money?" Kelly asked.

"I borrowed it from Peter Shanley."

"It looks like a good bet," Kelly remarked. "Hatch is determined to make me fight." He closed his eyes, and this time it was like shedding all the nerve strain. He began to sink into his weariness. He felt another robe being pulled over him and tucked in for warmth. His eyes drooped drowsily open. The rough wagon trip had had its way with Ellen's hair and there was something fresh and wholesome in its disorder. The first real gleam of daylight was touching her golden hair.

"You could sell it for sixteen dollars an ounce," he murmured. Then he was asleep.

They passed the last telegraph station late that night, and at daybreak they reached Jim Gamble's advance construction camp.

"We're out of poles," Gamble told Kelly, "but Barbas Brackett wired my east station yesterday that he's on his way

78

with a full crew. My west gang is still working this way along the Humboldt River, but they're about out of timber, too. I've got a hundred and ten miles of line to build. Can you get me the poles before you're snowed in up there?"

"That depends on how soon we get big snow," Kelly said.

The Rubies were in sight now, standing like a deep cloud on the horizon. There was snow on their high summits, but the lower reaches were still dark and beetling.

"I've got to depend on you," Jim Gamble said. "It's too late to get another contractor on the job this year."

Ellen had remained out of sight in the wagon during the stops at habitated places. She wasn't as indifferent to her reputation as she pretended.

Kelly drove the remainder of the distance. They reached the Brackett mill camp at the base of the Rubies late that afternoon. This camp was equipped with a stream-driven saw and planers to finish the poles and ready them for delivery. The majority of the mill crew had remained on the job, but they were idle, for no logs were coming down the mountain.

"Get ready for business," Kelly told them. "Barbas Brackett is a day behind us with the crew."

He and Ellen drove on up the rough, makeshift road that had been hacked up the mountainside. It climbed dizzily, crossing then re-crossing the series of skidways and chutes that had been built to speed delivery of the logs to the mill camp below. The faces of the skidways were sunburned, showing that no logs had slid down them for days or weeks.

Darkness was coming when they pulled up before a scatter of tents, grouped around the bigger bulk of a cook shack that was built of rough-hewn planks.

A handful of men appeared, and a lantern was flashed in their faces. "What's this?" a logger asked. "Ain't you Kelly

Brackett? Wasn't you here in camp fer a couple hours way back last summer?"

Kelly stepped over the wheel to the ground. "That's right," he said. "I'm back on the job now. How many of you bark peelers are here?"

They eyed him a moment. "Seven, countin' the cookie."

"How many sticks have you been sending down the mountain?"

Nobody wanted to answer that. "Hell," one finally said defensively, "we was told that Barbas had gone bust. We didn't know what to do."

"We're starting to hightail timber out of the mountains at daybreak," Kelly said. "At least you men stayed on the job. That means I can depend on you. Right? We've got more than four thousand poles to get to Jim Gamble's crews before snow buries us here." As he spoke, he was aware that the wind was raw and damp. The stars were invisible overhead.

A man said dubiously: "Looks like you're too late. It's goin' to be on us before mornin'."

X

"SHORT CREW"

The man was right. When Kelly rolled out of his blankets before daybreak, snow was coming down in a swirling flood. He rousted out the crew. "It may not last," he said. "But, snow or no snow, we're cutting timber."

He had made Ellen comfortable in a lean-to adjoining the cook shack. When he went into the shack to prod the cookie, he found her alone in the place. She had on a flannel shirt, blanket breeches, tuck boots, and wore a flour-sack apron and had a white cloth around her hair. She was working on a bowl of flapjack batter.

"I told the cook to report to the timber boss," she said. "I'm taking over the job."

Kelly indicated the driving snow that swirled through the lamplight beyond the open door. "How do you feel about your investment in Brackett and Company now?"

She said: "I wish I still had that money sewed up in my corset. Call the men. It's flapjacks, salt pork, and fried spuds."

The crew ate and watched the golden-haired cook with wonder. Then Kelly led them out into the snow, and into the timber.

He picked the huskiest man in the lot — a Swede with barn-door shoulders — for his partner, and started swinging a cross-cut. The others teamed up and followed his example.

Evergreens began going down with rhythmic regularity, for they were not after big timber. Then the snow suddenly tapered off, and the clouds lifted. The mountains were wrapped in a white mantle down to the 3,000-foot level below them, but there were only four inches of snow on the ground.

That reprieve from the weather lifted some of the moodiness from Kelly. He drove himself, drove the men until darkness stopped them. The first logs went down the skids. Jim Gamble's teamsters headed for the construction camp with their first poles in many days.

It was the following twilight when Kelly, walking back to camp, was elated to hear the sound of wagons on the trail. The main crew was arriving. He watched, frowning as only one freight wagon followed by a couple of mule wagons loaded with supplies pulled into camp.

A scant score of men clambered down into the snow. Barbas Brackett was lifted down, and he steadied himself on his crutches.

"Where's the rest of 'em?" Kelly asked, for there had been double that many loggers when he had left them pulling out of Salt Lake.

Barbas led the way aside, swinging grimly. "We was shot at from ambush before daylight after leavin' Salt Lake. A couple of wagons was stampeded an' wrecked, an' a logger was killed. Some of them quit an' went back on foot. More of 'em got cold feet this mornin' when they saw it had snowed up here. Luther Pritchard's honky-tonk looked a lot more cozy to 'em. They're down there at the bottom of the mountain takin' it easy in the Trail's End."

"The Trail's End?"

Barbas nodded. "We've got all the civilized refinements right within reach. The Trail's End has set up business down below. They moved the whole thing from Salt Lake by wagon. Passed us on the trail yesterday. They brung some painted women with 'em, an' two wagonloads of whiskey. They was set up for business, with the gals showin' their ankles an' the barkeeps offerin' free drinks, when we come along. Some of the boys looked at the snow up above an' decided they didn't want any part of it."

"Mike Hatch is down there, too," Galvin said significantly.

"An' Luther Pritchard in person," Barbas Brackett growled. "He's got a standin' offer of a winter's wages, free grub, an' likker to any logger who wants to sign up with him next spring."

Barbas looked old, beaten. "Hell, we can't get that timber cut before big snow comes," he said bitterly. "Not with a crew as short as this. An' we'll lose more. It's human nature.

Free booze, fancy women, an' pay without work. That's a tough combination to beat."

"Who's Pritchard got on his fighting string, outside of Hatch?" Kelly asked tersely.

"Plenty. I seen half a dozen or more of his toughs hangin' around. Likely he's got more'n was in sight."

Kelly led them toward the cook shack. Ellen, busy with the evening meal, had not had time to appear to meet the arrivals.

Robbie stopped short when she entered the cook shack. "Well, for pity's sake!" she exclaimed. "Miss Lash! I thought you were in Salt Lake."

"I arrived with Mister Brackett," Ellen said.

Robbie didn't get it for a moment. Then she straightened. "You came on that wagon with Kelly? Alone?" Robbie's mouth was severe, her sense of decorum shocked. She gave Kelly a nettled glance.

"Yes," Ellen said. "Though we weren't exactly alone. We had mules along and, sometimes, horses."

"I see," Robbie said stiffly.

Ellen said: "Call the men, Mister Brackett. Tell 'em to come and get it."

Afterward, when she had a chance to speak to Kelly alone, she said: "I'm sorry."

"For what?" Kelly asked.

"You care for Miss McDowell," she remarked. "And she thinks . . . well, I'll explain everything to her."

"Robbie isn't as narrow-minded as all that," Kelly snapped. "Just forget it."

Kelly found his chance to speak to Robbie presently. She had on a foxed suede coat that came to her knees, and it had a rich wolverine collar that set off the oval perfection of her face.

"I'll fix you up in the lean-to, with Ellen," he said.

"There's plenty of room. Barbas better bunk in the cook shack, too, for it'll be more comfortable for him."

Robbie said: "I detest that woman. Do I have to tell you how hurt I am, Kelly, that you . . . well, I wouldn't want to put it into words."

Kelly was startled, for Robbie was holding in her hands the ring that he hadn't seen since the day of the hold-up. She looked at him, and there was a softness and a forgiveness in her eyes now. "I don't know whether I have the right to wear this ring or not, Kelly," she said. "What should I do?"

She was close to him, looking up at him appealingly. Kelly waited for the old longing to sweep up inside him. She was so pretty. Then she settled it for him, and moved out of reach.

"That is something I'll decide for myself," she remarked.

Afterward, Kelly saddled a horse and rode down the mountain to the flats. He halted at a distance, looking at a lighted tent that stood alien and gaudy amid the loneliness of the sagebrush, the canvas slatting in the chill wind of the Ute desert. A fiddle was making music, and he heard the laughter of women. He rode soberly back up the mountain into the snow country.

When the crew turned out in the pre-dawn darkness, three of the crew who had come up the trail the previous night were missing. The allure of the Trail's End had been too much for them.

Two more deserted on the second night, and on the third day another foot of snow came down, clogging the logging trails, slowing the work. Poles continued to go down the skids, but Kelly saw now that it wouldn't be enough. Winter was at hand. He looked at the calendar. September 28th. Winter had held off overlong in the high country. Real snow might come any day now, any hour. Two more loggers had gone down the mountain under cover of darkness, convinced that the slave-driving work they had been enduring in the timber was futile.

Luther Pritchard evidently had been depending on the weather to win his fight for him, for none of his roughs had ventured up the mountain. Kelly had Peter Shanley and two other men he could depend on detailed as guards to patrol the mountain, but thus far they had seen no sign of trouble.

Galvin was in charge of the mill crew, but his real job was that of a trouble-shooter to see that the men were not molested down there. Robbie had taken over the bookwork and timekeeping in both camps. She came out to the timber often during the day, and spent much time in Kelly's company. She had not yet put his ring back on her finger, but the accusation that had been in her, no longer was there. Ellen slaved in the cook shack, and the tired loggers at least had no complaint about the meals.

The weather continued to hold off, and did so for five days. Logs were going down the mountain in a steady stream in spite of the short crew.

Then Luther Pritchard went into action.

XI

" 'LET'S GO!' "

It was past midnight and Kelly was sleeping in a lower bunk in a tent, along with six other men, when the roar of guns began rolling over the camp. Kelly hit the puncheon floor with the blood-chilling screech of bullets in his ears.

He yelled: "Down! Out of the bunks and down! Everybody!"

Always in his mind had been the fear that Luther Pritchard would call on his toughs to earn their money by some attack such as this. They had somehow managed to evade the man on night guard and were in the brush, shooting up the logging camp.

As a means of protection Kelly had lined the inner rim of the tents with a log barricade to a height of eighteen inches. His tent mates, one of them swearing and complaining that he had been grazed by a slug, came flooding from their bunks, flattening out in that shelter now, and he could hear the inmates of the two adjoining tents following suit. The storm of lead made a sieve of the canvas above their heads, but the men were beginning to shoot back now as they came out of their panic.

Then the red glare of flames made itself felt in the clearing. Kelly chanced a glance through the door. The cook shack was on fire, and he glimpsed a man diving back into the brush, casting aside a firebrand. The two girls and Barbas Brackett were in the cook shack, a growing mass of fire now. The odor of kerosene drifted in the wind. The bullets had covered the approach of the man who had soaked a wall of the shack with oil and touched it off. A chill wind was blowing, sweeping the flames toward the tents.

The loggers all recognized the situation simultaneously, even before Kelly yelled his warning. The majority of them had guns now, and they came swarming out of the tents, shooting into the brush.

The Pritchard gunmen didn't wait to fight it out. Evidently they had planned it this way. They had come mounted, for Kelly heard the crashing of hoofs in the snow-covered timber. Scattered gunfire flickered in the brush, but that part of the battle was over almost as swiftly as it had begun.

Kelly raced for the cook shack. As he reached the door, it

opened, letting out a blast of smoke and flame. Then Robbie came staggering out of that inferno almost into his arms. She was gagging and choking, and all she could do was to point weakly inside. Kelly turned her over to Peter Shanley, who had arrived. Kelly wrapped his arms around his head and leaped through the flames.

Only one wall seemed to be burning, but the interior was an oven. Kelly groped around, then heard someone coughing. In the next instant he came upon a woman's softness in the smoke. It was Ellen, and she was trying to drag Barbas Brackett toward the door.

"He's dead or wounded," she gasped. "Help me."

Kelly lifted his father's limp body, and pushed the girl ahead of him. Suddenly she stumbled and went down. He picked her up bodily under one arm, for she had succumbed to the smoke and heat. He staggered through the wall of flame that was following the draft through the open door, and fell on his face in the snow, dragging his father with him, and carrying Ellen like a sack of grain under his arm.

Helping hands rolled them in the snow, beating out the flames that smoldered in Ellen's flannel nightdress. Kelly revived quickly and began to help.

Ellen was reviving, too, but Barbas Brackett was unconscious. One of the bullets that had been fired at random through the walls of the cook shack had ricocheted from the stove, torn through a thin plank into the bunk where he was lying. The missile had been nearly spent, but it had struck him over the heart. It was flattened and had caused an ugly purple bruise, but the effect was more that of a knockout blow from a fist, for it had not penetrated his flesh. Then, slowly, Barbas Brackett began to come around. Ellen, her eyebrows and hair singed short, was sitting up now, wrapped in a blanket that Robbie had salvaged from one of the tents.

Kelly looked around. The tents were pyres of flames, puffing up as the wind had carried the fire from the fiercely burning cook shack to them. The storehouse adjoining the cook shack was in flames. The camp was wiped out. Their food supplies were destroyed, most of the clothing the men owned was gone up in smoke, and they were without shelter in a sorry-looking flat where the snow was dissolving into muddy pools beneath the heat of the fire. Two loggers had been wounded, and one of them had a bullet-shattered arm, but there were no dead men to bury.

Kelly felt something cold and hard against his cheek. It was snow. The wind was rising, also, and then it came, clamping down like a wall, dimming the crimson glow of the flames — a mountain blizzard.

Some of the cooler-headed men had managed to get enough clothing from the tents to cover them partly. They built a hasty brush shelter that gave some protection from the driving blast of snow, and Kelly looked grimly from face to face.

Galvin, who had come into camp that night, was present, and Robbie was sitting beside him. He appraised the others. There were only a dozen men left now, for two or three more, terrified by what had happened, had vanished and were on their way down the mountain. These remaining men were the toughest and best — the pick of the entire crew. And they were mad to the marrow.

"I'm going down to Trail's End," Kelly said tersely. "I'm going alone, if necessary. But any of you are welcome. If you're coming with me, bring your guns along and make up your minds to use them . . . but only if I give the word."

Galvin spoke with blazing fury. "It's about time. We'll shoot every damned rat that comes out of that hang-out."

Kelly looked at him. "No shooting unless I say so," he repeated. "We've still got a logging job to finish. We can't do it with dead men."

Galvin looked around ironically. "And you can't finish it with what live ones you've got left. A thousand poles to get out, and you'll have four feet of snow on the ground by dark tomorrow. This is real winter snow, or I never saw a mountain storm before."

"There are twenty, thirty men down at Trail's End husky enough to swing a saw," Kelly said. "There's only a dozen, or less, that'll really fight. The loggers likely will cave in easy. Pritchard's men are the ones we'll have to put the fear in. I'm planning on putting them to work. With that many men we can finish this job in a week, snow or no snow . . . if we're tough enough."

Barbas Brackett lifted a crutch above his head. "By God, that's the answer," he breathed.

Kelly said: "Are you with me, boys?"

They were with him — to a man. He grinned mirthlessly. "They've got grub down there, too. We'll need that. And that tent will shelter us, if we move it up here. Let's go!"

XII

"KELLY SINGS"

They descended the mountainside on foot, linked together with ropes to avoid being separated in the blizzard. They followed a foot trail down, rather than risk the wagon road that might be guarded by Pritchard's men. But the blizzard was an effective cover. The weight of the storm weakened as they reached lower levels, but the snow extended down to the flats, although here it was wet and soggy. It covered their advance on the Trail's End, which stood in the drifting storm like a drab and faded paper lantern, its pole and guy ropes outlined against the inner lamplight like ribs.

Kelly, moving at a long stride, marched to the entrance. A rough-mouthed man, who was standing on guard just inside the storm flap, gave a startled gasp and tried to lift a shotgun that he had leaning against the wall. Kelly kicked the gun out of reach, and shoved the man ahead of him. There were more than a score of men in the place, and he saw that many, who stood at the bar, were marked by their recent descent from the mountain through the snow.

Kelly's loggers were at his heels, and they spread out along the front wall, rifles and pistols lifted.

Kelly announced: "Freeze, everybody. Don't start anything or a lot of people will get hurt." He singled out three, painted women, and added: "You girls duck out the back way. Stay out of this."

Nobody moved for a moment. Mike Hatch was sitting at a table toward the back. And there was a bigger fish present. Luther Pritchard, wearing a fur-collared great coat, which hung unbuttoned, was sitting with Hatch at that table. More than half of the group were men who had quit the logging camp. A few others, evidently dead drunk, were sprawled in bunks back of a half partition of canvas at the rear.

It was the feminine mind that worked first. The women made a rush for a rear opening, which led to their quarters in a wagon.

Mike Hatch half turned, made a move as though to go for his gun.

Kelly said: "Easy, Mike. You're a long time dead."

Hatch shrugged and placed his hands slowly, carefully, flat on the table. He might have turned the place into a slaughterhouse if he had had the nerve. But his acquiescence was the turning point. Hatch said: "You like to have a gun in your hand when you brace a man, don't you?"

Kelly walked down the room, searched Hatch, and found a wicked spring-blade knife and a Navy pistol. "Line up at the bar, Mike," he ordered. Then he jerked Luther Pritchard to his feet. Pritchard had been sitting there, a sunken rage in his face. Kelly found a silver-mounted pistol on Pritchard. "A lady's gun," he remarked. He turned to the loggers, who were standing by, sheepish, uneasy, wondering what their part would be. "How'd you like to be on the end of a swing saw with Luther Pritchard bucking for you?" he asked ironically. "You're all going back to work, and Pritchard is going with us. In fact, we're all going to do some logging. Those who go willingly will be paid the usual wages. Otherwise, you'll work for nothing. But you'll work."

"You can't get away with this," Pritchard said, his voice thin as an overstrained violin wire.

"Line up!" Kelly ordered. "And keep your hands over your heads."

They began lining up. They had been caught off guard, and there was nothing they could do about it.

Kelly broke trail into camp when the blizzard blew out at noon the next day. Nearly three feet of snow lay on the level, and there were drifts that could swallow a horse and rider. Behind him came the recruits, guarded in pairs by armed men. Only Pritchard and his toughs needed prodding. The loggers were beginning to grin a little and to lick their chops in anticipation. The audacity of this stunt was beginning to appeal to their primitive natures, and they were ready to back Brackett & Company to the limit now. Pritchard and the toughs began to curse and balk when they were led into the snow-choked timber and saws and axes were placed in their hands.

Kelly walked among them. "You shot into a camp where men were sleeping," he said. "You fired a cook shack in which two girls and a crippled man were nearly burned alive. You shot up our wagons, killed a logger. I've been tortured with fire, shot at, and blackjacked. Do you think I'm going to be soft now? Get busy, or I'll peel the hides off every damned one of you."

Kelly had a bullwhip in his hand. He let the lash uncoil in the snow.

Mike Hatch, his little eyes blazing with helpless rage, picked up an axe and began swinging it. The others followed suit. Luther Pritchard looked like a man in a nightmare. His fine clothes were snow-caked, wrinkled. He was unshaven and he was scared.

Logs began to go down the skids. Men worked in snow that made every movement a double exertion. But they worked. The logs began going down to the mill camp in a steady stream before the day was over.

At night, armed men stood guard over the prisoners. The tent that had housed the Trail's End had been moved up the mountain on mule packs and offered shelter and stove-warmed respite from the cold. Food from the supplies that had been confiscated was served hot and piping. Ellen had the three painted women as assistants in the cook shack. Robbie would have nothing to do with those women and stayed in a smaller tent that had been put up for her comfort.

"We're slaves," Luther Pritchard sobbed at the end of the fourth day. "I'll see that you go to prison for life, Kelly."

"Any court in a civilized community would like to hear the whole story of this job," Kelly said. "Don't waste your breath, Pritchard. You know you don't dare go into court."

Kelly looked at the calendar. Jim Gamble's men had only a dozen miles of line to stretch on the desert below. Big clouds were massing about the peaks again. Another snow was coming, and this one would likely be too much to buck. It was October 15th.

He worked them that next day, driving them like a demon. It was mid-afternoon when he carved his initials on a clean spruce pole, and kicked it on its way down the skid. He looked at the entire group that had come in from the timber.

"That's it," he said. "The job is done. Overland Telegraph will finish its half of the line about the same time Pacific makes its hook-up on the eastern end, so Jim Gamble told me last night. The country will have wire service from coast to coast within a few days."

The loggers were cheering. The toughs were bitterly silent. Luther Pritchard was wind-blackened, leaner. He was cleaner physically, if not mentally. Mike Hatch hadn't had a drink in days and was probably in the best physical condition of his career.

But so was Kelly. He said to Galvin, who was standing with Robbie and his father: "You're going to lose that hundred, Lee."

"You can't beat him, Kelly. Why try? I'll call the bet off."

Kelly glanced questioningly at Ellen. She was thinner, but was still sturdy, self-possessed, and she was standing there alone as she always had.

She said quietly: "The bet was that you won the fight. But I want to call it off, too."

Kelly turned to Hatch. "Are you ready, Mike?"

"Do you have to do this?" Ellen asked wearily.

He nodded. "You know I do."

"I suppose so," she said, self-condemnation in her eyes. "And this time I'm the one that's helping drive you to it. It's your infernal pride. That's the only thing that has held you together through all this."

There was an area of packed snow at the head of the skid, level and offering good footing to hobbed boots.

Robbie left Galvin and tried to place herself between Kelly and Hatch. "Why continue this brutality, Kelly? You're not the man I've known in the past. You've become as hard and ruthless as the others. You're descending to Hatch's level, if you fight him."

Without raising her voice, Ellen said: "You little weakling, you drove him to this in the first place, you and your greediness that wanted to hold him to you, when you know that you love Lee Galvin. You still want to show your power over him, by trying to make him back out of this. Then you'll torture him by holding it against him in the future. Go and hide somewhere. You don't deserve to watch this. You aren't worthy of watching him. You never were."

Robbie backed away.

Kelly said to Ellen: "I fell in love with you somewhere along the trail. Maybe it was in the wagon."

All Ellen's warmth and fullness were there for him to see. "I put that white feather in my hope chest the night after the hold-up," she said. "I found it after they had searched you. And I've got that letter from the War Department that you were hunting. Your commission as a lieutenant of infantry is safe, along with the order detaching you from duty until the telegraph line was completed. The girl who pinned that white feather on you knows how wrong she was."

Hatch spat in the snow. "Better take a good look at him

now, lady," he promised. "You won't know him the next time you see him."

Kelly moved in on Hatch, and they crashed head-on, swinging. Kelly felt that black, heedless fury seething in him. He slugged Hatch in the face, took a punch in return. He evaded a kick in the groin, and they clenched. Hatch's thumb sought greedily for Kelly's eyeball, but he hooked his own thumb in a corner of the big man's mouth, instead, tearing a gash in his cheek. The pain of that forced Hatch to relax his grip an instant, and Kelly broke free.

They circled, came together again, and Kelly took punishment. Hatch was stronger, but Kelly was faster. Again Hatch locked arms around him, then shifted and sought to gouge. Kelly laughed, sank his teeth in a thumb till Hatch uttered a strangled sob of agony.

They fell, rolled over, and Kelly again broke Hatch's clutching grip. He half arose and leaped on Hatch with both knees. The breath gushed from the big man, but he held on again until his nausea passed.

Kelly finally broke away. They both arose, swinging. Kelly landed with left and right to the face, and Hatch's teeth splintered. A smash caught Kelly flush on the jaw and he went down. He rolled aside as Hatch leaped with his hobs to mangle his face, got to his feet, and was out of reach.

Kelly came in. He landed to the stomach, and Hatch began to cave. But the man lowered his head and charged like a bull. He drove Kelly back against the cribbing that guarded the skid, and Kelly felt his ribs bend under the impact. He survived that and kicked Hatch on the shins with his heavy boot, forcing the man away.

Kelly followed instantly, swinging again to the jaw. Mike Hatch was fish-mouthed, his lungs sobbing. Kelly sank a fist in Hatch's yielding belly. Hatch was going, but Kelly was about at the end of his strength, too, so terrific had been the pace. He braced himself and swung to the jaw. Hatch reeled back, stood there a tiny instant, and then his knees caved and he went down limply.

"Stomp him!" Barbas Brackett said harshly.

Kelly looked down at his victim. He turned away. Luther Pritchard was standing amid his silent toughs. Kelly swung a fist again, and Pritchard went down like a poled beef.

Kelly was blood-streaked, walking as in a dream. His father loomed before him. Barbas Brackett was saying: "Kelly! Kelly, my boy!"

Kelly said: "All right, Dad." But he pushed on past his father. There was only one person he wanted with him now. And she was there. He knew she would be.

Ellen's arms were around him, steadying him. He leaned his battered weight against her, and her strength and her softness were all that he needed.

"I'm with you, Kelly," she whispered. "Just lean against me. I'm with you, dear. I love you."

He held her jealously to him.

The Brave March West

"The Brave March West" was the author's original title for this much-reprinted story. The story was completed in February 1937 and sold the following month to Popular Publications. It was originally intended for the magazine, *Ace-High Western Stories*, but appeared instead as the cover story in the first issue of a new magazine, *Pioneer Western (8/37)*, under the title "Westward — to Blood and Glory!" The story was reprinted under an altered title, "Westward, the Wagon Trains!", in *.44 Western (11/51)*. Under its original magazine title, the story was included in the Western Writers of America anthology, *Western Bonanza: Eight Short Novels of the West* (Doubleday, 1969), edited by Todhunter Ballard. It won the 1970 WWA Spur Award for best Western short fiction of the preceding year. The story was reprinted again in the *WWA* anthology, *Spurs* (Bantam, 1977). From its opening on a plague-ridden steamboat on the Missouri River to the conclusion at the gold fields of California, this is an action-filled, heroic, but intensely human story of an epic cross-country journey and of the profound effects of this journey on the small group of people who undertake it.

A steamboat whistle growled hoarsely through the night mist below the Trailville landing. For a moment the sound seemed to galvanize the crowd that filled the rude town square.

The oncoming craft became an indistinct gray blur through the fog that lay over the murky Missouri. As though that were a signal for action, the distorted shadows of men in Conestoga boots and round-brimmed felt hats writhed across the background of log and unpainted plank walls, and the crowd surged down the bank to the river's margin.

The resinous tang of bubbling pitch torches met the muddy dankness of the river. The swaying crimson glow struck without warmth on the muzzle of the brass cannon that sweating volunteers wheeled into a position where it could sweep the landing. A stodgy man with a tobacco-stained beard, wearing a nickel-plated star on his butternut shirt, gave orders in an excited, asthmatic wheeze, and amateur gunners rammed powder and a load of grapeshot home.

Women in wide dresses and shawls came, clutching children close, to stand anxiously on the low bluff. But their presence laid no softening influence on the purpose of the massed, sullen men below.

The steamboat was a twin-wheeled craft. Her paddles gave forth a watery booming as she poked her prow uncertainly through the mist. She showed her black-lettered name on a wheel-box as she swerved clumsily, and a mutter ran through the waiting crowd.

Join the Western Book Club and GET 4 FREE* BOOKS NOW!
A $19.96 VALUE!

Yes! I want to subscribe to the Western Book Club.

Please send me my **4 FREE* BOOKS**. I have enclosed $2.00 for shipping/handling. Each month I'll receive the four newest Leisure Western selections to preview for 10 days. If I decide to keep them, I will pay the Special Members Only discounted price of just $3.36 each, a total of $13.44, plus $2.00 shipping/handling ($19.50 US in Canada). This is a **SAVINGS OF AT LEAST $6.00** off the bookstore price. There is no minimum number of books I must buy, and I may cancel the program at any time. In any case, the **4 FREE* BOOKS** are mine to keep.

*In Canada, add $5.00 shipping/handling per order for the first shipment. For all future shipments to Canada, the cost of membership is $16.25 US, which includes shipping and handling. (All payments must be made in US dollars.)

NAME: _____

ADDRESS: _____

CITY: _____ **STATE:** _____

COUNTRY: _____ **ZIP:** _____

TELEPHONE: _____

E-MAIL: _____

SIGNATURE: _____

If under 18, Parent or Guardian must sign. Terms, prices, and conditions subject to change. Subscription subject to acceptance. Dorchester Publishing reserves the right to reject any order or cancel any subscription.

"It's her," the wheezy, bearded man said hoarsely. "The *James Madison*. You got to back me up in this, boys. I'm only carryin' out instructions."

The *James Madison* was riding low under the weight of a top-heavy deckload. Pittsburgh and Conestoga prairie wagons, glimmering in their fresh red and blue paint, their tall white tilts untarnished, were lashed hub to hub on the lower deck. Cargo mounded the passenger promenades and overflowed to the texas deck. And from her depths came steady lowing of chained cattle.

Unskilled hands were at the wheel. The *James Madison* bucked the current haltingly as conflicting signals changed below. There was weariness and desperation in the way the laden boat staggered ponderously toward the torch-lit landing.

The bearded man's thick fingers shook as he picked up a muzzleloading rifle. He looked to the crowd again, with a plea for support, then lifted the gun and sent a shot across the bow of the laboring steamboat.

"Sheer off!" he bellowed. "You ain't welcome at Trailville. There's no room for you here. This here is Milt Walters, town constable of Trailville, speakin', an' carryin' out the command of the council meetin'."

The warning echoed emptily against the sounding board of the dark river. A few faces appeared at the rails of the steamboat, standing gray and indistinct in the outer reaches of the torchlight.

A man leaped from the pilot house, and ran to stand in full view on the top deck, staring. He was in white shirt sleeves. His dark hair reached back from a high forehead, accentuating the untanned hue of his face. He cupped his hands. "This boat is carrying sick and dying humans!" he yelled. "There are women and children here in need of urgent help, as well as men. We must demand that you give us assistance."

Constable Milt Walters stood aside, so as to reveal the gaping maw of the cannon.

"Sheer off, I tell you," he bawled, "or we'll sink you an' your blasted load of death! We know what you got there . . . a pesthouse of cholera. A rider come up the Independence trail only two hours ago to warn us. We ain't aimin' to let you turn the plague loose here in Trailville. We got women an' kids to think about here, too. Hundreds of 'em! There's three hundred wagons camped here, outfittin' fer Californy an' Oregon. Go back to Independence or Saint Louis, where you come from. Pull out in the river, I say."

A second man joined the one on the top deck. He was a deep-chested, tow-headed giant, whose big fists were knotted like mauls.

"You slobberin', snivelin' cowards!" he boomed, his voice rolling and breaking against the walls of the town. "You ain't turnin' us away. There's twenty bodies on the deck below that need decent burial, an' there's half a hundred sick an' dyin' in the cabin, with only a handful of us able to care for 'em. The pilot an' the captain are dead, an' we ain't got enough hands to load wood or keep the boilers goin'. We're landin' here an' *demandin'* help. I'll bust the neck of any weasel-minded coward that tries to stop us."

Milt Walters snatched a torch from the hand of a bystander. He leaped to the fused cannon, swinging it to bear on the steamboat.

"Back off, damn you!" he screeched. "Or I'll put a load of grape through your boilers!"

The two men stared, stunned and incredulous. The tow-headed giant turned to seize up a rifle, but the white-shirted man stopped him.

"Steady, Toby," the latter muttered. "They mean business. They're not in their right minds. We've got to reason with them."

He turned and issued a crisp order to the man at the wheel. A bell *clanged* in the engine room, and the *James Madison* brought to a stop. The boat's prow swung away from the landing, and her paddles held her there against the current, fifty yards clear of the rude wharf.

The dark-haired man cupped his hands. "I'm Clyde Rhoades of Boston, doctor of medicine!" he shouted. "In the name of humanity, listen to reason. We must have help at once. There aren't enough of us to care for the sick and to man the boat. Most of the crew have deserted or are in the sick bay. We're short of fuel. We'll never reach Saint Joe without help, and we can't get back to Independence. We must appeal to you in our extremity."

Milt Walters rubbed small, cold sweat from his pasty brow, looking around at the massed crowd. "Anybody want to volunteer to go out to that boat?" he asked shrilly.

A dead silence followed. There was a nervous shifting of feet, and men did not dare to meet each other's eyes. Gray faces stared blankly back at the whiskery constable. Here and there a few men made a half-hearted effort to step forward. But instantly the hands of friends drew them violently back.

A woman came racing down to the landing, and caught the arm of her husband, who had started to move stubbornly forward. "You ain't goin' to sacrifice yourself, Ben!" she screamed frantically. "You'll git the plague sure . . . an' die. What about me? What about the children? You ain't takin' your life that way. What would we do if we was left alone here in this god-forsaken desert?"

The man faltered, and the woman drew him back into the security of the waiting crowd.

Cholera! The thought of it was like a drug that held them

chained. In the throng were brave men and compassionate women, who would carry to their graves regret for this moment of selfishness. But now they were gripped by the horror of the great plague that had devastated the Mississippi river towns and was relentlessly spreading up its great tributaries.

There was cholera in Independence, the historic starting point of the great trails; caravans bound for the Promised Land, which the discovery of gold at Sutter's Mill had opened the previous season, were driving westward madly in the hope of escaping it. There was cholera at St. Joseph, the last port up the river. But Trailville, created by enterprising land speculators between these two points, was as yet free of the malady.

Clyde Rhoades spoke with vast scorn. "Do you mean to say there's not a man among the hundreds of you who will help sick and dying humans?"

The sullen mass of men remained silent under that indictment. Then from the crowd a tall, commanding figure moved. He was a stern-faced man with frosty eyes and long, waxed mustache, garbed tastefully in long, gray broadcloth coat and beaver hat.

He lifted a hand. "Have patience, my friend," he said curtly. "Perhaps there are ways of helping you."

He turned to the constable, lowering his voice. "You have some prisoners in the jail house, Walters," he stated. "No doubt, they would be glad to accept freedom in return for manning that boat until it gets to Saint Joseph."

Milt Walters had a slow mind. He shook his head. "There ain't one of 'em but what would rather go to the whippin' post, Colonel," he said reluctantly.

"Use your brains, man!" the stern-faced colonel snapped impatiently. "The choice won't be left to them. They don't need to know that cholera is raging on that boat."

Walters's heavy face began to lighten. He rammed a fist exultantly into a palm. "By godfrey, Colonel!" he rasped. "You've hit the nail on the head. Le' me see. I got two Indians in the calaboose for bein' drunk. They was given six months in the chain gang, an' we need 'em to work on the roads, but I reckon the council will let 'em go. An' there's that Memphis gambler an' a muleskinner, who was to git five lashes for desecratin' the Sabbath." He paused, looking triumphantly at the colonel. "An' there's that white Indian, Zeke Rust, who goes to the whippin' post tomorrow for twenty an' one for. . . ."

"Not Rust," the gray-haired colonel snapped imperiously. "I demand that he receive his punishment. He assaulted two of my bullwhackers, beat them unmercifully, and put them in the care of a doctor. He attacked me bodily. He's nothing but a raw barbarian, even though he is of the white race. He deserves no consideration."

The constable's face fell. "Beggin' your pardon, Colonel Renfro," he argued with meek deference. "But Zeke Rust knows the river. He likely kin pilot that pest boat safe to Saint Joe, an' git 'em off our hands. He's been up an' down the river, as well as the Californy trail, since he was born. Besides, I'd like to git shet of him. He damn' near took the jail house apart this evenin'. I had to give him a flask of rum from my own pocket, which stretched him out dead drunk, or he'd have busted loose an' started rippin' the town apart ag'in. He's worse'n a pack of Pawnees when he goes on a tear." Then the constable winked, and added: "Maybe, Colonel, you'll run across him somewhere between here an' Californy, an' carry out the sentence. Rust is sure to go out with a caravan as soon as he's finished his spree. He don't stay long in the settlements. Of course, he might go under with the cholera. You are takin' that chance."

Colonel Cooper Renfro stood considering that. He was a big man, conscious of his importance as the captain of a caravan of forty wagons that was outfitting for the long trail. He liked to be addressed by his military title, which he had acquired while serving as adjutant on the staff of the Rhode Island home guard during the Mexican War.

Abruptly he nodded. "I'll forego my demand for Rust's immediate punishment, Walters, and will entertain the hope of encountering him again."

Milt Walters drafted the help of a dozen husky men, and lumbered up the ramp to the Trailville jail, a low, log-built structure set in a swamp away from the cramped buildings of the frontier town. Presently they prodded into the torchlight two reeling, stupefied Iowa bucks in grimy, wrinkled blankets and greasy buckskins. A shoddy, tinhorn river gambler in disheveled, rusty black coat was pushed sullenly along in the company of a teamster in homespun and seamy trail boots.

Muscular bullwhackers carried the last prisoner from the jail. His long, raw-boned body dangled limply between them, as they panted under his weight. His head hung back, and his mouth gaped open as he snored heavily. His fingers were still wrapped around an empty rum flask. Dried blood and discolored bruises mottled his face. Except for his long, unkempt sandy hair and long-jawed, aquiline features, he might have been mistaken for another Indian. His weathered buckskin breeches were shrunken six inches up his lank, freckled bare shins. He wore a stained hunting shirt and parfleche moccasins of a manufacture not recognized by these men familiar with the tribes of the Eastern prairies. A Nez Percé squaw had chewed the soles and drawn the sinews for his garb in some lodge up in the shadow of the Tetons, a thousand miles away in an untrailed wilderness.

"Scum!" Colonel Cooper Renfro pronounced, caustic scorn in his voice.

Women drew back fearfully as the mountain man was carried by. They breathed easier after Zeke Rust had been laid on the prow of the steamboat, which was allowed to run its plank ashore to take on the prisoner.

Only two men handled Zeke Rust now, but it had taken five slab-muscled drovers and river men to take him to the jail house that afternoon. The wild mountain man, fresh from the long trails, had wrecked a tavern and sent two opponents to the hospital in a rough-and-tumble battle against overwhelming odds. He had thrown Colonel Cooper Renfro into a horse trough as a climax to his spree, and had paid for that by being dragged before the magistrate and sentenced to the whipping post at dawn.

"There's your crew!" Milt Walters shouted as the drunken Indians and bewildered gambler and freighter were hustled up the plank. "Sheer off! If any of you try to come ashore, you'll be shot down."

Clyde Rhoades stood straight and accusing on the top deck. "You crawling worms!" he spoke bitterly. "You can go to your beds tonight with the knowledge that you've sentenced suffering humans to certain death. We'll sheer off. If we live through this, we'll see to it that white men will hang their heads whenever the name of Trailville is mentioned. And if any of you cowards cross our trail on the way to California, we'll make you remember this night."

The paddles began to churn. The *James Madison* backed slowly away from the Trailville landing.

The tinhorn gambler had been standing on the prow, staring and listening. Suddenly he comprehended the meaning of all this. He uttered a hoarse cry of horror. "Cholera!" He screamed and shook frenzied fists at the crowd on the landing.

"Damn you, you've put me on a plague ship!" Suddenly he leaped to the rail and down into the river. His head emerged, dimly visible in the receding glimmer of the torches on the landing. He struck out frantically. Then a churning paddle wheel sucked him under. He did not appear again.

The grimy muleskinner had also pulled himself to the rail, ready to leap. He stayed there, staring, then shrank back, whispering: "A plague boat." He sobbed. "I'm a doomed man."

The two flat-faced Iowas stood woodenly, their bloodshot eyes dull and uncomprehending. They did not understand the white men's language.

And Zeke Rust lay where they had dropped him on the prow, his long, sinewy arms and legs sprawling loosely. The towering tilts of the lashed prairie wagons loomed high above him. He snored on, oblivious of the destiny that had saved him from the whipping post and placed him aboard a craft whose cargo was death and suffering.

II

Four men came hurrying down to the lower deck and found their way along the wagons to the prow. Clyde Rhoades, the young doctor from Boston, looked at the blanketed Indians and at the cowering drover. His dark eyes narrowed.

"Two filthy Indians and a weasel-faced white man. And what's this sick man lying here? An Indian by his looks. No, he's of white blood." Rhoades bent closer, then stood up with a grimace. "He's dead drunk."

He took the empty flask from Zeke Rust's hand, hurled it into the river. "Blanket Indians and drunken whites!" he gritted. "The dregs of the town. They must have emptied their jail to turn these men over to us."

The tow-headed giant, who had roared his defiance to the people of Trailville, sent the cowering muleskinner and the Indians hustling aft.

"Git into the fire room an' keep them boilers hot," he spat. "Now that you've been wished onto us, we'll make you try to act like real men."

Vibrant power ran in the towhead's deep voice. He was under thirty, as handsome as a Hercules, with his deep chest and lithe brawn. His name was Toby Swan. The love of the soil was in his blood. His palms were callused deeply, for he had come from an Illinois farm answering the siren call of the gold trail to the Western mountains. Stored in his wagon were dismantled plows and harrows, and seed corn and wheat. If the miner's pick failed him, Toby Swan meant to take his gold from the fertile California land with the plow.

The beacons on the Trailville landing were vanishing around a bend as the *James Madison* steamed uncertainly upstream at half speed. The hull grated on a sandbar, lurched slightly. The four men stood rigid, staring tensely at each other. Then they pulled breath deep into their lungs again as the craft worked free.

"We've got to find a pilot who knows the river," one of them said. "Else we'll hang up on a bar, or rip out her bottom on a snag."

The speaker had a terse, practical tone. He was blocky of shoulder, of medium height, and wore the black, square-toed shoes and fustian garb of a trader. Waldo Magoffin, from Ohio, was heading for California with a Conestoga-load of merchandise that should bring high prices in the new mining camps. In the back of his mind plans were already forming for setting up a chain of trading stores on the Pacific Coast.

Lee Fitzpatrick, the fourth man in the group, was straight as a pine, tall, good-looking, with reckless, proud features and cool gray eyes. Fitzpatrick had been a lieutenant of dragoons under Scott in Mexico. The thin white scar across his cheek bone was a memento of the assault upon Chapultepec Castle. Fitzpatrick had the long, sensitive hands of a gambler and the spirit of a soldier of fortune. He was fastidiously garbed in belled gray hat and a waistcoat, with white linen stock and fawn-colored trousers. Like the others, his face showed exhaustion.

He stirred Zeke Rust's body with a scornful boot, and spoke with the soft drawl of the South. "Perhaps this white Indian can handle the wheel, gentlemen. He's full of rum at present, but he can be aroused."

Fitzpatrick dipped a bucket into the river, and sloshed the muddy water over the mountain man. He repeated the process until Zeke Rust began to stir and mumble.

Rhoades brought his medical bag, and bent over Rust with a bottle of castor oil. The mountain man gagged as the greasy concoction touched his throat. He sat up groggily, clutched at a wagon wheel, and dragged himself to his lank height. With a mighty effort he reeled to the rail and doubled over it, retching and gagging.

Finally he began to mumble weird oaths in the jargon of the mountain men. He straightened weakly. His three-day growth of sandy whiskers was stiff as bristles. He focused his bloodshot eyes on the four men, then took in the dark rush of the river and the clanking of the paddle wheels.

"Steamboat, hey?" he muttered. "How in the blue tarnation did Zeke Rust git aboard this tub?"

Clyde Rhoades answered in his aristocratic accent. "You

were put aboard by the citizens of Trailville. Evidently you were not consulted, so I'll be frank with you. We are badly in need of a pilot who knows the river. Cholera is raging on this boat." Rhoades paused, waiting to see Zeke Rust's reaction to that.

"Yeah. What about it?" Rust growled indifferently.

"There are only a dozen able-bodied men aboard," Rhoades snapped, not liking the fellow's insolent tone. "Practically all the crew, except the engineer, are dead or have deserted. Trailville refused us any assistance."

Rust looked back at the faint glow of lights below the bend that marked Trailville. "Yuh might have known them dough bellies would show their yellow," he stated.

"If you know the river, in God's name take the wheel," Rhoades pleaded.

Rust spat cotton from his puffed, fist-marked lips, and looked at the cargo of covered wagons. "Immigrants an' gold-grubbers, hey!" he remarked with high aversion. "Flockin' like moon-eyed sheep into a clean country with your plagues an' dirty civilization! It's in my mind thet mebby the Almighty brought the plague on yuh to keep yuh back where yuh belong. Last year it was the smallpox that the 'Forty-Niners carried with 'em. This season it's the cholera. No wonder the tribes are dancin' an' poisonin' their arrows."

The boat shuddered again, staggering the men. Zeke Rust reeled groggily against a wagon wheel. He turned a glance at the opaque darkness, seeming to sniff the foggy dankness of the river. "Port!" he roared, his voice carrying all through the boat. "You're pilin' her on a mudbank. Climb that wheel, yuh blasted flathead. Port! To the left, damn your hide! Don't yuh know which side of a boat is port? D'yuh want to hang her up for keeps?"

The amateur helmsman heard that command and obeyed

with frantic haste. Once more the *James Madison* labored free, her paddles churning thick mud astern.

"I perceive, sir, that you do know the river," Lee Fitzpatrick drawled. "We would consider it a great favor if you would take over the helm personally."

Zeke Rust ran a raw-boned hand over his cracked, peeling lips. "I ain't of a mind for goin' to Saint Joe," he declared positively. "I got some business to take care of back in that blasted mud hole astern. They jumped me, six of 'em, an' used knuckle dusters an' wagon spokes on me after I had dowsed a high-nosed billy goat into a horse trough for crowdin' me offen the sidewalk. I'd ha' cleaned 'em single-handed if they'd fought bare-knuckled, like men. I'm goin' back to take some bark offen them, d'yuh hear!"

"We'll pay you well," Waldo Magoffin spoke up tersely. "I'll start the purse with a hundred in gold specie."

Zeke Rust laughed jeeringly. "Gold? Hell, I dug that stuff with a Bowie knife from a mountainside in Californy only this spring. Blowed it in on foofaraw an' rum an' the Vide Poche gals in Saint Louey. Now I'm headin' back to dig me some more."

Magoffin stared. "You mean to say you've already been to California . . . and found gold?"

"Why not?" Rust snorted.

There was doubt in their faces. Zeke Rust did not appear any older than any of them.

A feminine voice sounded, choked and desperate. And they heard running feet on the deck.

"Clyde! Clyde Rhoades! In the name of heaven, where are you?"

A bareheaded girl darted among the wagons and came into the lantern light on the prow. She caught Rhoades's arm with frantic strength.

"It's Mother," she panted. "She's . . . she's. . . . Oh, I'm afraid! Please hurry, Clyde."

Her tear-moist eyes were tragic brown pools against the sensitive refinement of her features. She was small, and Zeke Rust had a feeling that there was a bewildered, terror-stricken child playing at grown-up in her full-skirted, tightly bodiced dress. But there was curving fullness in her figure and womanly depth in her voice.

"Courage, Sue," Rhoades said, and hurried away, an arm around her slender waist.

Toby Swan looked at Fitzpatrick and Magoffin quickly and challengingly. Then the three of them followed, leaving Zeke Rust forgotten.

Rust stared scornfully after them. He was still sick and unsteady on his feet. He looked at the dark shoreline that slid slowly by. The west bank of the Missouri was well within reach for a strong swimmer. Rust moved to the rail. He paused there. He had never come to the end of his endurance in the water; it was not lack of faith in himself that caused him to pause. He shrugged, muttered something that sounded like an impatient oath, then turned and stalked among the wagons in pursuit of the girl and the four men.

He mounted the companionway to the passenger deck. There he hesitated as though he had encountered an invisible barrier. Slowly his unshaven jaws went tight as he stared through the windows into the passenger lounge. From that dimly lighted place came a steady, fearsome sound — the respiration and the slow moaning of two score cholera sufferers.

The patients were lined up on mattresses and blanket beds on the floor of the cabin. Some of them were tossing in weak delirium, and a few hopeless, exhausted men and women moved among them, seeking to allay their misery.

In the dim darkness of the foredeck, a space had been cleared of cargo. There, in a row, lay canvas-shrouded bodies. Zeke Rust began counting the dead — but he quit with a shudder when the toll had reached a dozen.

Moving mechanically, he stepped into the sick bay. The brown-eyed girl and the four men were grouped around a patient, and Rust moved mechanically closer, his moccasins making no sound.

The girl had knelt and was pressing her cheek against the wasted face of a woman. In spite of the ravages of the plague, there was resemblance between them. The girl's mother was dying. Zeke Rust had seen death too often to be mistaken. Again he ran the back of his hand over his mouth, and felt his senses draw fine as he listened to the gasping breathing of the older woman. The sound broke, caught again once or twice, then faded out and was not heard again.

There was a space of silence. Then Rhoades touched the girl's shoulder gently. She looked up wildly, searching his face. Her eyes turned hopelessly back to her mother. She came to her feet numbly.

"Clyde?" she choked. "Oh, Clyde!" That was all. She buried her face against his linen shirt, and her body was taut with restrained grief.

Zeke Rust heard the keel scrape faintly on a bar or snag. He pivoted and ran out, mounting to the pilot house like a shaggy cat. He pushed aside the middle-aged farmer who had been doing his best at the wheel.

"Git down below an' help with the sick, sodbuster," the mountain man snarled. "That's all you're fit for."

He craned his neck through the pilot house window, sniffing as though he was smelling out the channel through the opaque blackness of the river. The wheel spun violently in his hands. Soon he rang for full speed, and the *James Madison* picked up momentum, her prow slicing keenly through the black current.

Rust was still there, leaning out into the misty darkness, smelling out the course, when Rhoades and Toby Swan climbed wearily to the pilot house an hour later.

"Shake up them shirkers in the boiler room," Rust grated at Swan. "We're losin' steam."

Swan spread helpless hands. "They deserted ten minutes ago," he growled. "Jumped overboard when we rounded that last bend, as my back was turned. We're out of fuel, anyway. We've got to land somewhere."

"When your back was turned, hey?" Rust jeered. "I reckon you was too busy worryin' about that little brown-eyed heifer that lost her maw tonight to 'tend to business. It was your job to keep them rats on the boat. But I seen the way you looked when she buried her nose in the doctor's shirt. You was green with jealousy, mister. It was in your eyes."

Toby Swan's broad features went white beneath their tan, and he took an angry step toward the mountain man. "Blast your hide! For a pin, I'd maul you," he growled. "I'm aimin' on askin' Sue Hatfield to marry me someday, an' if you ever so much as talk about her, I'll bust you in pieces."

Zeke Rust laughed raucously. "Damn me, if I don't reckon yuh'd put up a purty good ruckus, even if you have got the earmarks of a plow pusher. So yuh aim to wed her, hey? 'Pears to me you've got competition. She acted right partial to the doctor here. An' I happen to notice that the dude from Virginy an' the box-jawed pilgrim with the big gold watch chain sorta hung close around."

Toby Swan's big fists had knotted, but Rhoades interfered. "None of that, Swan," he said curtly. "I'll admit, he deserves it, but this isn't the time. Rust, we must land somewhere. Steam is about gone. We're losing headway."

Zeke Rust bent a contemptuous glance at him. "Go back to your patients, mister," he said. "I'm already headin' her to shore. I been lookin' for a good spot ever since I seen them Injuns an' that muleskinner jump overboard. If I'd had a rifle, they wouldn't have made it."

The paddles were turning only weakly now. A yellowish blue of shoreline loomed up sluggishly. The *James Madison*'s hull crunched solidly into sand. The craft lurched a little, with a creaking and settling of the cargo. Then she lay still, grounded within reach of dry land.

Rust turned from the wheel. "Git 'em ashore," he commanded. "They'll be better off out in clean air an' sunshine than cooped up in this pesthole. We'll git some fires goin', an' bed 'em down on that sandbar. Git busy!"

Resentment at his assumption of command blazed in their faces, and they paused, glaring at him challengingly. Then Rhoades, with a faint smile of futility, shrugged, and they turned to obey.

III

In the light of blazing brush fires, forty afflicted humans were carried ashore and made comfortable on bedding brought from the steamboat. The river fog had gone. Stars blazed down from a prairie sky. The fresh coolness of grass and clean distances came in on the west wind.

Clyde Rhoades had the increasing impression that he had gained a powerful ally in his fight against the plague. Zeke Rust, eyes bloodshot and lips dry as an aftermath of his spree, matched even Toby Swan's strength in the work.

The shadow of his wild, buckskin-clad figure passed ceaselessly against the firelight as he helped with the sick and carried supplies ashore. His blunt, intolerant tongue stabbed at patients who had given up hope, aroused them to a sort of anger that brought life back within their reach. He treated them as he did the plague itself — with lofty contempt. It was plain that the mountain man considered them as interlopers, weak of body and spirit, and to be merely tolerated and treated as helpless children.

"You'll have to go back to Indiany, an' shuck corn an' feed pigs, pilgrim," he told more than one man who had given himself up to the ravages of the plague. "It's a danged sight safer'n what you'll find if you go beyond South Pass. There's things in that country that'll turn your hair white overnight."

His eyes fell upon Sue Hatfield. She had given way at last to nerve strain and grief, and had sunk down on a drift log in the shadows, burying her face in her hands.

Rust strode to her, lifted her roughly to her feet. "There's stew pots ready for the fire," he said curtly, as though he was addressing a squaw. "Some of these fellers could stand a little beef broth. Git busy."

A hand caught his shoulder and whirled him. He found himself facing Lee Fitzpatrick. The Virginian's gray eyes were blazing.

"You trail bum!" the Southerner gritted. "Keep your filthy hands off her. You're not among Indians now. She's a white woman, so far above you that you're not fit to breathe the same air with her."

Zeke Rust had light blue eyes, and they turned to chilled granite. Then Sue rushed between the two men, pushing Fitzpatrick back.

"No, no, Lee!" she implored. She turned on Rust, her eyes

115

flashing. "You . . . you raw, ignorant savage!" she raged. "I've watched the way you've been acting. What right have you to patronize men like Lee Fitzpatrick or Clyde Rhoades? Or Waldo Magoffin and Toby Swan? They've been more than two days without sleep or rest of any kind, fighting to save lives, while you lay in some frontier jail in a drunken stupor. They're men! Real men! And I demand that you keep a civil tongue in your head when you refer to them."

Zeke Rust was grinning faintly. "Maybe yuh won't call 'em that by the time they git to Californy . . . if they got the sand to make it," he jeered. "Sleep! Why, ma'am, they don't know what bein' tired is. They'll learn if they go over the long trail."

She turned away, trembling, and ignored him after that. But she failed to squelch him.

"Pert little filly, ain't she?" Rust remarked loudly. "No wonder every young blood in the outfit is squabblin' for her favor."

Clyde Rhoades arose from ministering to a dying man. "Rust," he said, and his fine voice bit like a lash, "you are taking advantage of our situation to insult men and women. But if you ever speak of Miss Hatfield again in those terms, I'll kill you."

Zeke Rust's grin died. Something entirely wild and ruthlessly primitive showed in his face. "I'll take a lot of killin', Doctor," he said softly. "Always remember that."

He looked around. Toby Swan was glaring balefully at him. Waldo Magoffin was standing in heavy silence, his eyes hard upon the mountain man. Zeke Rust surveyed them, one by one, with cool challenge. He smiled coldly and took a deep pull from a tin cup of rum.

The tension passed. Sue Hatfield, her cheeks burning, turned to tend the cook fires. Her apathy and grief were forgotten in the heat of her resentment. And Rust's attitude aroused the weary men, drove them to emulate his own tireless, ceaseless labor in sheer defiance. Some of the weight of disaster and death was forgotten as they squirmed under his domineering manner.

It was not until dawn that it occurred to Clyde Rhoades that he was at the end of his endurance. He looked around before he went to sleep. Big Toby Swan was stretched out by a fire, overtaken by exhaustion. Magoffin and Fitzpatrick were asleep, too. The patients had quieted. Only Zeke Rust moved among them, watching, carrying fresh water, arranging blankets over fretful, tossing forms.

Cholera strikes swiftly. . . . And its tale of life or death is soon told. For a week the plague took its toll there on the dry sand spit on the west bank of the Missouri, where the great prairies come down to the river. Then one morning Clyde Rhoades drew a long breath. With no new cases for two days, he knew it had run its course.

There were thirty graves in the flat of wild sunflowers. Nearly eighty passengers of the *James Madison* were alive and convalescing. Passing steamboats had stopped to offer help. Two more doctors were with them now, giving Rhoades the chance to rest. The story of Trailville's disgrace had gone up and down the river, and the news came that enraged immigrants had wrecked the new river town, tarred and feathered Milt Walters, and sent the town councilmen into hiding.

Zeke Rust listened to that tale of vengeance with a disgusted expression. "Why in blazes wasn't I there to see the fun?" he complained. "Did they catch a coot that calls himself Colonel Renfro?"

"Renfro is on his way to California with forty wagons," he

117

was told. "But it ain't likely nobody would tar him, anyway. They say he's a bigwig in politics back East."

"I'll find him somewhere," Rust murmured.

A serious meeting was held around the council fire at night on the sandbar. The wagon parties aboard the *James Madison* had formed a solid unit. In St. Louis they had taken a pledge to cling together through the long trek to the gold country. But the ravages of the plague had left men discouraged. Wives were without husbands, sons without fathers. The company was broken up, and many of the survivors had already turned back to Independence.

Clyde Rhoades, acting as captain, stood by the blazing fire, tall and distinguished.

"Many of you are turning back, I know," he said. "But some of us are going on. Toby Swan, Lee Fitzpatrick, Waldo Magoffin, and myself are determined to go over the trail in spite of the lateness of the season. There is a possibility that we may be turned back by winter before we cross the Sierras. We mean to make every effort to make up for the delay that has occurred. We recognize the dangers, however, and we are willing to chance them."

His eyes sought out Sue Hatfield in the crowd. "Miss Hatfield, who lost her mother and her teamster in the plague, will go with us . . . if she can hire a man to handle her wagon and stock. Her father, as many of you know, is in California, where he is representing the government in the problems arising from the formation of the new state, and she is determined to join him as soon as possible, in spite of the danger.

"Any more who wish to accompany us are welcome . . . but they must have adequate equipment. Seven yoke of oxen, instead of the previous five yoke, has been set as a minimum. And nothing but new Pittsburghs or Conestogas will be permitted. Inferior equipment cannot be accepted. Disaster to one wagon may mean disaster to us all . . . for we have agreed to stick together, come what may."

Zeke Rust had been sitting on a wagon tongue in the background, not having been invited to take part in the council.

"Rhoades, yuh forgot to mention that the Sioux an' the Utes are beginnin' to raid the trail," he said casually.

Rhoades shrugged. "There have been rumors of Indian trouble, but I discount them. Indians did not bother the caravans last year. There is no reason to believe they will cause trouble for us."

Rust arose. "The Injuns are beginnin' to wake up to what they stand to lose," he stated slowly. "A white man was a curiosity to 'em in 'Forty-Nine. This year they're realizin' he's a pest that kills their game, robs 'em of their land. Yuh'll have to fight to git to Californy, d'yuh hear?"

Rust's eyes turned to Sue Hatfield. "I never seen a white woman's scalp dryin' in a lodge," he added grimly. "It wouldn't be a pleasant sight. My advice to you pilgrims is to wait till next year, an' go out with the big caravans."

Sue Hatfield stepped forward, color beginning to rise in her cheeks, and walked to Clyde Rhoades's side. "Nothing can turn me back," she said clearly. "My father is expecting me, expecting my mother. I want to be the one who tells him about . . . about what happened to her."

Zeke Rust came walking indolently into the circle now, his ragged moccasins scuffing the sand. "I'll care for your wagon an' bulls, miss," he said casually. "You furnish the grub, an' I'll call it square as far as wages go. Since you're determined to reach Californy this year, I suppose you'll be wantin' a drover."

Sue Hatfield looked embarrassed. "Why, why. . . . That is, I didn't think you wanted to go with us," she said. She turned to the crowd, hoping some man other than this wild mountaineer would offer his services. But there was no response. Stories had come back about a boggy trail and Indian trouble on the plains. Two caravans had passed within sight of the camp, heading back to Independence, discouraged by conditions ahead.

She was forced to turn to Rust. "Do you know the trail?" she asked weakly.

"Born in sight of it in a Crow lodge. My mother was the first white woman to start for Oregon by wagon. She died the day I was born, an' my dad never came back from a buffalo hunt. The Blackfeet got him. I was raised at Fort Hall in the Shoshone country. I've been to Oregon an' I've been to Californy. I've been over the *Jornada* from Santa Fé, across the southern desert to a pueblo called San Diego, where whalin' ships put in. That's in Californy, too, but it's a long ways from the mines. Yes, miss, I know the trail."

The names that he spoke in such a matter-of-fact tone were of places remote and known only by hearsay to these stampeders from beyond the Mississippi.

Sue Hatfield still hesitated. She was glad of the interruption that came. The hoofs of trotting horses sounded, drawing the attention of the meeting.

From the darkness of the prairie, six riders appeared, halting within reach of the firelight.

Zeke Rust stepped back, and his hand went to a pistol that he had bought from a wagon man. The leader of the arrivals was the stern-jowled wagon captain, Cooper Renfro. With him, riding saddle mules, were five husky bullwhackers, armed with rifles and belt guns.

Renfro dismounted, drawing a silver-mounted cap-and-ball pistol. There was a thin smile of satisfaction in his lips. "I learned only today that I would find this man here," he said, indicating Rust. He jerked his head. "Put the irons on him, boys."

Zeke Rust did not move. "Come on, you dough bellies," he said softly. "Try an' take me!"

"Just a minute," Clyde Rhoades rasped sharply, and moved to face Renfro. "What's the meaning of all this?"

"This man, Zeke Rust, savagely attacked and maimed two of my employees some time ago," Renfro explained. "He was sentenced to twenty and one by the magistrate at Trailville. I mean to see that he receives his punishment."

"And who are you?" Rhoades asked coldly.

"Colonel Cooper Renfro, captain of a company of forty wagons, sir. We are returning to Independence, deeming the trip across the great desert impossible at this time, in view of the lateness of the season. I will take this man, Rust, back to the jurisdiction of civilized law, where he will be dealt with."

"Get on your horse and clear out of camp, Renfro," Rhoades snapped. "Zeke Rust, whatever he is, worked with us here, helped save lives, slaved to dig graves for the dead, braved the cholera. You're not taking him."

"Not by a hell of a sight!" boomed Toby Swan, at Rhoades's side, a rifle in his big hands.

Lee Fitzpatrick's hand moved and came up with a brace of short-muzzled pistols. Waldo Magoffin picked up a double-barreled buckshot gun with matter-of-fact deliberation.

Renfro, startled, stepped back hastily, lowering his gun. "You realize that you're shielding a criminal?" he blustered.

Rhoades pointed to the horse. "Ride, before we tar and feather you," he snapped. "I remember you now. I saw you on the Trailville landing the night the *James Madison* asked for humane assistance."

Zeke Rust pushed past them, scowling. "I kin fight my own battles without help from any soft-handed pilgrims!" he raged. "Stand back, damn yuh fer a pack of interferin' fools! I'll make this turkey buzzard an' his beagles eat dirt."

121

Cooper Renfro retreated before the enraged mountain man and turned to board his horse. But Rust's moccasin caught him, lifting him violently before he reached the saddle. The animal bolted then, and Renfro was glad to head it out of camp into the darkness of the prairie. His five men swung their mules and followed without looking back.

Rust turned and glared around. "If yuh ever dip your bills into my fun ag'in, I'll hold yuh for it," he frothed.

His glance fell upon Sue Hatfield. She was just hiding away in her shawl a ball pistol that she had drawn. The wrath ebbed suddenly from Rust. Slow blood built a coppery tinge in her sun-darkened, fierce face. Half abashed, half puzzled, his glance wandered back to the four men. There was something like incredulity in his expression.

Clyde Rhoades spoke. "You did us a big favor, Rust. We aren't entirely ungrateful."

"Let it rest there," Rust growled. His eyes turned toward the darkness of the prairie. The night wind was laden with the promise of the green short-grass country immediately to the west, of streams and wild sunflowers and growing grass. But Rust's mind was leaping far beyond the middle prairies, over the Continental Divide. He was seeing the wastes of sage and lava hills, the glint of alkali flats under a burning sun, with saw-toothed mountains remote and forbidding in the distance.

Once more he looked at them questioningly. "We'll see if your sand holds out that far," he muttered, and he stalked away.

They did not know what he was talking about. They were to learn that later.

Rust moved to the wagon owned by Sue Hatfield. He inspected it critically. With a little annoyed frown, she realized that he was taking for granted her acceptance of his offer to serve as her drover. She looked at the four men and smiled a little ruefully. Her voice was oddly soft. "He's the only one who seems willing to go," she murmured apologetically. "And I haven't the heart to refuse him. He'd go back to Independence and get into trouble. After all, he fought through the plague with us."

When Toby Swan saw his chance, he herded her away from the crowd to the seclusion of the cottonwood shadow beyond the wagons. The tow-headed giant was awkward and nervous. He took a long time in getting around to what was uppermost in his mind.

"Sue," he finally blurted out huskily, "you know how I feel about you. I'm a farmer, a sodbuster, horny-handed, an' none too strong on education, but . . . but . . . oh, hell!"

She stood looking up at him, a little tender smile framing her mouth, curving it into lush sweetness. "I understand, Toby," she said softly, and her eyes became bright. "You're trying to tell me that you love me."

His big hands enclosed hers gingerly as though he feared he might crush them. "Is . . . is there any chance for me, Sue?" he whispered huskily.

She remained broodingly silent for a long time. "I don't know," she admitted. "Any woman would be proud to be your wife, Toby. I'm proud to have you ask me. But . . . I don't know . . . yet."

Swan's big face lost some of its vital hope, and his lips went hard with disappointment.

"Is it Clyde Rhoades?" he demanded. "Or maybe Lee or Waldo?"

She seemed weary and at a loss. "I don't know," she repeated hopelessly. "Sometimes I think I love all four of you too much to choose. You're wonderful, every one of you . . . brave and good and generous."

"Then some of 'em has asked you, too?"

She smiled wanly. "All of them. That's what makes it so difficult. If only there were four of me . . . or one of you, I'd be happier."

Toby's hopes revived. "Then I've got as good a chance as the next one." He grinned. "We're hittin' the long trail soon. You'll be marryin' one of us when we reach California, Sue. I aim to be that lucky man."

A banjo began to tinkle by the wagon fire. They went back. It was Lee Fitzpatrick playing. In his drawling baritone he sang the plaintive, brave song that had come to typify the spirit and the soul of those who went over the great trail:

> **Oh, Susannah, don't you cry for me,**
> **I'm off to California with my banjo on my knee.**

Sue's clear contralto and Toby Swan's rolling bass joined in, picking up the anthem of the California trail.

Zeke Rust slouched against a wagon wheel, shadowed by a great arched canvas tilt. The firelight played fitfully on his bronzed, hawk-like face as he listened. He heard the song, and he was attentive to the far lonely response of coyotes, whose lament came forlornly down the wind — like a challenge.

IV

The lumbering wagons halted, and Zeke Rust strode forward, dragging the bullwhip. He stood, with hands on his lean hips, studying the North Platte. The river was high and swift. As the girl and the four men joined him, he saw the dismay in their faces.

"She's up an' still risin'," Rust commented casually. "But there's a shallow bar leadin' acrost at this point, unless she's been washed out since last year. Mebby it ain't so high but what we can still ford the wagons. I'll saddle up the mule an' see what our chances are."

They eyed the river dubiously. Driftwood was rolling on the surface, following the margins of the stream. Here and there oily, long whorls of deep brown mud came spinning to the surface, sucking flotsam under.

"Two of us better go," Clyde Rhoades said quietly, and began saddling his black gelding.

Sue Hatfield's face was troubled. "It . . . it's dangerous," she breathed. "Perhaps we had better build rafts."

"That will take time, Sue," Rhoades explained. "We must ford it if it's at all possible. Every day counts."

She stood with Toby Swan and Magoffin, tense and fearful, as the two mounted and rode down to the margin of the rising river. Somewhere on the trail Rust had bought a saddle mule from discouraged Argonauts who were turning back. And, at a friendly Arapaho village, he had outfitted himself with new fringed buckskin breeches, a hunting shirt of unborn elk-skin, and moccasins dyed to suit his love of vivid color.

Sue Hatfield was beginning to understand why the tribes and white men of the plains dressed colorfully. It gave them escape from the drab monotony of a changeless land. Cold rain squalls swept the river now, veiling in cheerless mist the rocky, sterile plains. The short-grass country was behind them, and they were mounting to the great plateau of rock and sandy wastes and sage.

The four mud-caked wagons were nothing more than

125

wheeled mounds that formed a part of the gray-green mono-tone. Here along the river, brush and cottonwoods gave some relief to the eye, but even the flooding Platte seemed lost in the overpowering weight of the land.

Canvas tops drooped over the bows, resembling the ribs of the work-worn oxen. The top on Swan's Conestoga, wrecked by a prairie hurricane back in the Pawnee country, was patched and tattered.

Eight hundred miles of trail lay between them and the sand spit where they had buried the plague victims. It was a wet year on the mid-prairies. Steady, chill rains had turned the trail into a morass of gumbo mud. Magoffin had lost one span of oxen during those weeks of wallowing.

At Zeke Rust's insistence, they had abandoned the main trail. Blazing a new route, Rust had found firmer traveling during the past week, but the time was already late July — and South Pass, the halfway point to California, still lay somewhere ahead of them.

They had encountered many wagon trains turning back, acknowledging that California could not be reached ahead of the Sierra winter. Rust was thinking of the Sierras as he rode down to test the ford. He was recalling the fate of the Donner party a few years previous in those great granite vastnesses.

He looked at Rhoades doubtfully. "The stream's a little r'ily, an' that's a fact," he remarked. "Mebby you better let me try it first. It ain't exactly a jog for a greenhorn."

Six weeks of association had brought no understanding between them. Rust still seemed to consider them weaklings and intruders in an untarnished land. He treated them with indifferent tolerance while teaching them the ways of the trail.

Rhoades eyed him coldly, then urged his mount into the water. He had to use steel, for the animal did not like the aspect of the broad sweep of rolling river ahead.

Rust shrugged and followed. Side-by-side, they forced the animals out from shore. The current sucked at the legs of the mounts, came to their stirrups, then swirled and splashed against saddle skirts.

"Take it easy," Rust cautioned sharply when they were more than a hundred yards from land. "Yuh might step off into a hole. Deep water just below. Yuh'd have to swim for it if. . . ."

Rhoades's horse, a length ahead, lurched, tried to rear back — and failed. It went completely under. When it reappeared, the current had swept it yards downstream. The saddle was empty. The horse floundered, began swimming, as the river swept it into deeper water.

Rust leaped to his feet, balancing himself on the saddle of the mule, scanning the surface. Rhoades's head came above water downstream. He was splashing wildly. There was the grim resignation of a doomed man in the brief glimpse Rust had of his face. Then he sank back again.

Sue Hatfield's frantic scream ran piercingly over the river: 'He can't swim! He's drowning!"

Cursing, Rust sent his long body diving in a distance-covering plunge downstream. He came up swimming, his shoulders streaking through the muddy water. Rhoades, struggling weakly, rolled sluggishly to the surface just ahead of him, then sank again. Rust went under, swimming down. His reaching hands locked on the drowning man's hair; he fought his way to the surface and swung Rhoades's head clear.

They were drifting with the current far below the ford. As Rust began stroking toward the shore, he could see Swan and Magoffin and the girl racing down the bank with coils of rope. Then minutes later they were dragged to land nearly a quarter of a mile below the ford. Rust's lips were ashen, his muscles shaking from the effort, but he helped Swan turn the

127

limp body of the young doctor over a deadfall. They pumped the water from Rhoades's lungs, and Fitzpatrick knelt and, with his mouth, forced respiration and life back into the unconscious man.

Rhoades began breathing normally after a time. His eyes opened. Rust was squatting near on his moccasin heels, scowling darkly.

"Why didn't yuh tell me yuh couldn't swim?" he demanded.

Rhoades smiled weakly. "Bull-headed, maybe," he conceded. "I'm tired of having you make out that you're a better man than me."

There was a thoughtful frown on Rust's face as they went back to the wagons. Now and then he eyed Rhoades covertly. Grudgingly he was forced to admit in his heart that maybe there was some fiber in this pallid-skinned, studious doctor with the aristocratic accent and fastidious manners.

They cut timber, built a raft, and floated the wagons across the Platte. That cost them four days. Two oxen drowned in trying to swim the river.

V

The mud and rain became only a memory as they toiled up the valley of the Sweetwater, past Independence Rock, through Devil's Gate, and on to the Continental Divide. August heat lay searingly on the land as they wheeled their wagons over South Pass into the headwaters of streams whose destination was the Pacific Ocean.

Now Rust could find no game to fortify their provisions. The main range of the buffalo lay behind them, and the gold stampede that had passed over the trail ahead seemed to have blotted out all wildlife or harried it far off the route.

They had passed the Pawnee and Sioux country. Those tribes were at war; they had no time to molest the white travelers. But ahead lay the Shoshones and Blackfeet and Paiutes.

Except for their own crawling progress, the great trail lay deserted. Even the occasional caravan of discouraged Argonauts, who had turned back to the Missouri settlements, had ceased.

Rust began to drive them now, stretching the wagons out before dawn, keeping them on the trail until exhaustion of the oxen forced outspanning long after dark.

Sue Hatfield would hear him prowling the camp at all hours of the night, like a restless animal scenting danger. And at each halt on the trail he would ride away with his rifle, declaring that he was hunting game. But all of them knew there was no game in the country.

Rust kept his own counsel. The absence of other wagons on the trail had a significance that only he comprehended. Twice he had crossed the trails of mounted Shoshones. There had been no squaws with them. They might be hunting parties. Then again they might be wearing war paint.

Fort Hall, on the Snake River, was their immediate goal. There they would provision the wagons for the long march across the Humboldt Desert and fill out their depleted ox teams.

Sue Hatfield kept counting every slow mile to Fort Hall. She envisioned at least a day of respite from the maddening monotony of plodding oxen, the dust, the endless creak and lurch of the rumbling wagon, when they reached the post of the fur company on the Snake. She longed to have a day in feminine dress again, for she had long since abandoned skirts for the more practical garb of overalls, shirt, and round felt hat.

She began to envy Zeke Rust's wiry endurance and his stony indifference to the hardships and toil. He treated her with a distant respect, which she believed was dislike. She still resented his attitude. Once when Magoffin, through clumsy handling, came within an ace of capsizing his wagon on a rocky slant, she heard Rust mutter something scornfully about "penny-grubbin' lard-eaters". "Lard-eaters" was the sobriquet the mountain men reserved for clerks and tradesmen.

There was constant friction between Rust and Lee Fitzpatrick. More than once the proud Virginian had been on the verge of challenging Rust to a duel. Only Rhoades's counsel had deterred him.

Rust looked upon Toby Swan with a trifle more tolerance. He still placed Swan in the category of a greenhorn and an interloper, but he was forced to admire the towhead's massive strength. Physical prowess seemed to be the only thing he could understand.

Rust's attitude toward Clyde Rhoades puzzled Sue. Since that episode on the Platte, he had had little to say to the Boston doctor. Occasionally she imagined there was a hint of deference in his manner toward Rhoades.

Rhoades had brought in his wagon a small library of classics for his own diversion. One evening when Rhoades was on stock guard, Sue accidentally came upon Rust with a book that the doctor had been reading. The mountain man was absorbed in the volume, his lean finger moving along the lines, his lips forming the words silently. He closed the book with a snap as he discovered her presence. He came to his feet with a flash of resentment.

"Rust, where did you learn to read?" she asked in surprise.

"Father DeSmet, the Jesuit missionary amongst the tribes, tried to give me learnin'," he said curtly. "But I reckon it didn't take."

He strolled away with elaborate unconcern. But afterward it seemed to Sue that Rust had employed less and less of his mountain jargon in his brief conversations.

The dry heat of late August blanketed the wide, sage-dotted valley of the Snake River as they came in sight of Fort Hall. Rust brought the pilot wagon to a stop, and stood there like a man turned to bronze, his eyes suddenly flat and hard.

Sue felt sharp disappointment as she stared. She had built a hopeful picture of an imposing stone fort, tree-shaded, with armed sentries on the bastions, surrounded by a peaceful, busy village. The Fort Hall of reality was a drab, mud structure on the gray flats, uninviting, almost forbidding in its aspect.

Rust turned and looked at them. "Abandoned!" he stated laconically.

They stared at him blankly. For the first time, they realized that there was no sign of life about the fort. The disaster struck slowly at them, for at first they could not believe the truth. Then the numbness of it came over them.

"Why, in God's name?" Clyde Rhoades blurted out. "We were to provision here. We've got to buy food here."

Rust shrugged. "Stretch out," he snapped impatiently. "We'll quit the main trail from here on."

"Just a minute!" Fitzpatrick spoke up sharply. "Why should we quit the trail, sir? We may lose our way, wander for days in the. . . ."

"You fool!" Rust snorted. "Can't yuh savvy the things that lay right before your eyes. It's death to follow this trail now.

131

This country has been swept clean by the Indians. That's why the fort's empty. . . . Look!"

Half a mile beyond the fort they discovered a black dot against the silvery sage. As they drove closer, they made out the staggered bows and burned fragments of wagons. Buzzards fluttered up from the débris, and the raucous hubbub of their wrangling came faintly to their ears.

Rust saw Sue Hatfield turn deathly pale. "We must do what Rust says," she said suddenly, and her courageous voice belied the pallor in her face. "That caravan was much larger than ours."

Rust eyed them. "Yuh could turn back," he suggested. "It ain't too late yet. There's always another year, yuh know."

"Not by a damned sight!" Toby Swan spoke up. "We're more'n halfway to California. We're goin' on. You kin go back, Rust, if you want. There's no call for you to risk it. None of these wagons belongs to you."

Rust grinned at him, spat scornfully. "It ain't only the Indians that makes it tough," he remarked. "We're just startin' the real trail now."

And his bullwhip sang and cracked. Now they understood what he had meant back there on the banks of the Missouri when he wondered how long their sand would hold out.

"I'll handle the wagons," Sue spoke up. "You will have enough to do, Rust, in scouting the route."

She took the whip from his hands, and he did not oppose her. She knew the art of bullwhacking. He had taught her.

As Rust rode ahead of the wagons, he looked back occasionally. And there was a hopeless smolder in his blue eyes. He would glance down at his weathered, shrunken buckskin garb, then mentally compare himself with Clyde Rhoades, who maintained a clean-shaven freshness even in the rough cotton and wool garb of the trail. But when he looked back, it was not at Rhoades, but at the boyish figure that was handling the lumbering bull team in the lead.

Rust piloted them into rolling sage country a dozen miles south of the main trail, uncut by man-made wheels. Swales and basins helped mask their progress there.

On the second day, riding ahead late in the afternoon, Rust suddenly slid from the mule, then led it hurriedly to cover in a coulée. He tethered it and went wriggling on knees and stomach to the rise of a swell, where he lay motionless among the hot, odorous sagebrush. The wagons were more than a mile behind.

Rust saw movement among the sage wastes north of the dry creekbed the wagons were following. An Indian crawled away, mounted a pony that had been hidden in some depression, and dusted away through the sage. After a time Rust saw a line of riders move like a string of ants across the sun-seared plain two miles north. He counted twelve warriors and judged that they were Shoshones. He lay there a long time, sighting them at intervals. Following what cover the plain offered, the Indians were swinging in a semicircle ahead to intercept the route of the wagons.

When he was certain of their intention, Rust crawled back to the mule and returned to the wagon. "We're throwin' off," he announced tersely. "There's water here . . . enough to take care of the cattle for the night."

Fitzpatrick made an impatient gesture. "It's still two hours till sundown, sir," he protested. "We can do a few more miles. This is a poor camp spot."

"Shoshones," Rust said bluntly, with a jerk of his head to the west. "We've been sighted. They're aimin' to ambush us in that stand of rocks you see ahead. They don't know that I sighted 'em. We'll pick our own ground for the fight, an' hope that they come to us."

He dismounted, looking grimly from face to face. "It's a small scoutin' party. I counted a dozen. I'm hopin' that they're young warriors, ambitious to count coup. Our only hope is to tempt 'em into jumpin' us here where we camp. We ought to be able to handle a dozen, now that we're fore-warned."

VI

At Rust's insistence, they made their usual type of camp, turning the oxen out to grass without a guard. But as soon as darkness came, they worked feverishly. They brought the cattle inside the square formed by the wagons and chained them to wheels. Then they dug a trench a few rods beyond the wagons. It commanded the entire expanse of dry riverbed. Rust scattered the excess dirt, so that it would not destroy their position in the darkness.

"Injuns generally wait till daybreak," he declared. "Keep your heads down. Use your ears."

Rust was the only one of the six who slept. He would awake at intervals to listen, then drop asleep again. Five rifles and a shotgun stood loaded and ready in the ditch, in addition to six cap-and-ball pistols.

The night was timeless. As Sue listened to the restless stomping of the oxen and to the far lament of coyotes, she placed a hand in Magoffin's square, reassuring palm, and leaned her head against Kirkpatrick's shoulder.

"At least, if we die, we shall all die together," she murmured.

"No talk," Rust's guarded voice came at her in a harsh command. Even her whisper had awakened him.

Rust came awake after midnight and slept no more. He squatted with Indian patience in the darkness, without sound or motion, until the girl felt like screaming to ease the tension in her own body.

A vague dimming of the stars was the first hint of the coming day. Then Rust moved silently, picking up a rifle.

"Steady!" he told them, his voice a mere sigh. "Pick up your guns. No sound! There's plenty of time. They're out there."

After a time he lifted his head by inches until his eyes cleared the lip of the trench. The luminous pallor that was neither day nor night showed the dark dots of sage here and there on the yellow flat. And it showed other dark dots that moved slowly toward the bulky outline of the wagons.

He counted them. Twelve warriors. One by one, he touched the four men and pointed out targets. "I'll give the word to fire. Hold your bead true. The odds are tough enough as it is. Think about the girl here. Don't let them devils take her."

Gun barrels slid over the trench. The Shoshones were in a ragged, open line, crawling swiftly, seeking to take the wagons by complete surprise.

"Now," Rust said calmly.

Muzzles flamed with a deep bellow, sending black powder smoke swirling. The scream and wail of dying red men sounded through the startled war whoop that burst across the dawn. These Indians failed to leap to their feet. The nine survivors milled for a moment, then rallied and came racing upon the trench, howling and shooting.

The Shoshones were a proud race of fighting men. Two of their number went down under the hammering lead in that charge. Then they swarmed into the trench, swinging tomahawks and knives.

Rust sent his last bullet into the chest of a breech-clouted brave. He saw a sinewy warrior lunging at Clyde Rhoades, with a long knife raised. Rust's gun barrel shattered the Indian's skull. The flat side of a tomahawk glanced from Rust's head, staggering him. He felt blood gush down his face. He whirled, dove low, flipping the Indian over his shoulder. He spun about again and leaped, his gun barrel rising and falling relentlessly.

Fighting Indians and panting white men fell over him in the narrow trench. A coppery form leaped on his back, clamping his arms. At the same instant another Shoshone reared up before him, swinging a tomahawk.

Rust could not evade that weapon. But as it descended, the tall figure of Lee Fitzpatrick, arms dangling uselessly from the effects of wounds, dove violently against the Indian. Fitzpatrick would not stop that descending tomahawk, but he collided with the warrior and diverted the blow — upon himself. The gleaming blade bit deeply into his shoulder.

Toby Swan, like a great infuriated grizzly, caught the Shoshone by the throat, then broke his neck with an explosive wrench, and hurled him from the trench.

Rust felt the arms of the warrior who still clung to his back go limp as Clyde Rhoades struck with an axe.

A rifle *boomed* in the trench. A warrior, who had leaped to escape from the gory ditch, threw up his arms in convulsive silhouette against the gray eastern dawn, then fell back. Sue Hatfield had fired the shot from a gun that she had managed to reload in the midst of the shambles.

Rust, an axe in his hand, looked dazedly around through the blood that streamed from his scalp wound. An incredible silence had come. Dead and dying Indians choked the ditch.

The Shoshone scouting party was wiped out. There were no survivors — none to send for reinforcements.

Lee Fitzpatrick lay among them, covered with blood. Rhoades was clutching a slashed arm, staring about numbly. Toby Swan, with a scalping knife still dangling from a shoulder muscle, lifted Sue Hatfield to the rim of the ditch. Magoffin stood stanching a gash from his chest.

Rust picked up Lee Fitzpatrick in his arms, climbed out of the gory ditch.

"Rhoades!" he rasped. "Pull yourself together. Fitzpatrick's hurt . . . bad! He saved my life. Took the hatchet that was meant for me. You've got to pull him through. Move, damn yuh! Fitzpatrick was willin' to die to save me . . . me that he despised. I ain't goin' to let him die."

Zeke Rust, who had just killed four Indians, was almost sobbing as he hurried to the wagons with the unconscious ex-soldier. Fitzpatrick had a bullet-broken arm and two deep tomahawk wounds.

Rust sat for hours beside the blanket bed in the shade of a wagon, watching every move as Rhoades fought to fan the spark of life in the Southerner. When Rhoades finally nodded and said there was a chance, Rust arose and walked away by himself, silenced by emotion.

Bandaged, still in their blood-stained garb, they inspanned and drove out of the massacre camp at noon. Sue rode in the wagon with Lee Fitzpatrick, soothing his delirium.

At dawn, two days later, they camped in heavy brush on a small stream. They remained there two weeks until Fitzpatrick was well on his way to recovery. Then they struck south along the trail that would lead them into the Humboldt Desert. Already they were rationing flour and beans and fortifying their menu with the stringy meat of jack rabbits.

Rust shot two more oxen, to end their suffering. They had three span left, emaciated, hollow-eyed creatures that were no more than animated effigies of hide and bones. The lone remaining wagon was empty, except for Lee Fitzpatrick, who was not yet fully recovered from his wounds of six weeks earlier.

Magoffin's Conestoga-load of trade goods had been abandoned far back on the Humboldt Desert. Toby Swan's plows and his wagon were mired in a salt slough miles inland. The seed corn and wheat had long been eaten by oxen and humans. All that any of them possessed now were the ragged clothes on their backs and a few firearms.

They had not eaten in two days. Only a scant half gallon of water remained in the wagon barrel. Once they had tried to eat the flesh of oxen, but the toxic poison in the exhausted animals had sickened and weakened them.

The wheels crunched alkali and plowed through feathery volcanic ash, stirring up choking dust. In the sandy stretches the four gaunt men put their shoulders to the wheel to help the feeble cattle. Sometimes the girl, whose eyes were sunken and enlarged abnormally, helped push the load.

Carson Sink, with it alkali *playas* that gave a mocking mirage of water in the distance, its clear, blinding sun and gaunt desolation, was a gigantic treadmill beneath their raw, swollen feet.

Rust walked beside the oxen, inspecting every abandoned piece of equipment that dotted the trail, hoping, as he had hoped for days, that he would find food. There were anvils and picks and furniture, a baby's cradle, trunks of finery — the odds and ends of civilized existence here in Carson Sink. But there was no food or water.

Far ahead loomed mountains. The Sierras of the Promised Land of gold and sunshine! Their saw-tooth rims faded away against the sky into a luminous, indistinct white mist.

Sue's dull eyes noticed that phenomenon. "What is that above the mountains?" she asked indifferently.

"Clouds," he assured her swiftly.

They plodded on. As the morning advanced, the mountains faded into the shimmering sun-glare ahead. Waldo Magoffin, his heavy lips puffed and dry, waited until Sue was out of hearing, then spoke gruffly to Rust.

"That's one lie you won't be held for on Judgment Day, Rust. That wasn't clouds over the mountains, and you know it. It's snow on the high summits. The Sierra winter is setting in. I felt the cold bite through me last night."

"Don't tell her, Magoffin," Rust said quietly. "She's got enough to worry about. An' one snow don't make a winter."

Magoffin nodded, trudged on. He stumbled over a tiny wind ridge in the baked alkali, went heavily to his knees. He reeled after he got to his feet, but he set his jaw and plodded on.

Rust eyed him gravely. "How'd you like a long, cool drink of water," he asked, "like that we got from that trout stream above Green River a couple months ago?"

Magoffin turned on him like a tiger. "Damn you, Rust!" he snarled, and a touch of madness flickered in his haggard face. "Isn't it bad enough, without you taunting me? I dreamed about that stream last night. I can't get it out of my mind."

"Then why did you slip your ration of water back in the barrel this mornin', instead of drinkin' it?" Rust spat.

Their eyes met hard. "I'll ask you the same question," Magoffin countered. "I was watching you, Rust."

Rust lost patience. "Yuh mule-headed fool! Yuh sneaked back your ration so the girl an' Fitzpatrick would have more. Yuh ain't foolin' me any."

"And why did you go without water?" Magoffin snapped.

Rust had no rebuttal for that brand of logic. He walked on, the futile bullwhip coiled around his neck. He began appraising the stocky Ohioan with quick, wondering glances from his red-rimmed eyes. In all the long weeks on the trail there had been nothing in common between them. Magoffin was a man of crowded cities, not understanding the plains and desert, with no desire to learn.

The next time Magoffin stumbled to his knees, Rust helped him arise. In the afternoon Magoffin began to fall often and mumble, staring vacantly ahead.

Rust motioned Toby Swan then. They seized Magoffin, placed him in the wagon, tied him hand and foot, forced water down his swollen throat. Even then he opposed them, pleading half deliriously to save the water for the girl and the weakened Southerner.

At last he quieted and slept like a child. Rust squatted there on his moccasined heels. "Yuh stubborn, lard-eatin' son," he murmured to himself, and there was something vastly tender in his tone. "Yuh got sand aplenty, ain't you?"

He looked up at Sue, and she saw the wistfulness in his eyes. Absently his gaze roved to Clyde Rhoades, emaciated and ragged, but still unbeaten. And to Toby Swan, shaggy as a bear, and as invincible.

"You're a lucky girl," Rust spoke softly. "No matter what happens, you can know that you've had what few women are lucky enough to possess. Four men that. . . ."

He left it unfinished, and dropped from the wagon. His bullwhip *cracked,* and they lurched forward.

The last drinkable water of the Humboldt River was far behind them. What water they saw was in alkali-crusted pools, too saline even for the thirst-maddened oxen. Somewhere ahead were the Truckee Meadows, where Rust said they would find green grass and clear, rushing water.

"There'll be rabbits there, an' ducks," he told them. "We'll eat an' drink!"

Abandoned wagons and the carcasses of dead men, mummified by the desert sun, landmarked the route as far as the eyes could carry into the quivering distance.

At sunset, Rust doled out the last of the water, giving the oxen triple the human share.

"We're not campin'," he announced. "The cattle won't ever rise ag'in, if they once bed. If we don't make it to the meadows come sunup, the story is told."

They shambled on as the remote stars came through a cold velvet sky. Rust's arm steadied Sue Hatfield in the yielding salt crusts. Unconsciously she began to lean more and more upon his strength.

When she realized it, she drew away from him. "Rust," she said hoarsely, "why do you stay with us? You're strong enough to get through alone. We have no claim on you. I want you to go ahead."

She could see the fierce lift of his head.

"What!" he grated. "Leave you? Leave them?"

She felt the weight of his accusation. It occurred to her that all the old scorn and arrogance was gone from him. Suddenly she came to realize that she understood Zeke Rust. It was plain to her now that his lusty wildness, his blunt ways and intolerance, had been an armor, assumed as a shield against the ways and knowledge of strangers like herself who came from what, to him, was another world — a complicated world of civilization, which puzzled and frightened him.

She looked up at him. "Rust, if you get through this alive, what lies ahead for you? I mean . . . what are your plans?"

He turned to peer at her. He assayed a jeering laugh. "First, I'll get drunk," he declared. "Then I'll hunt for gold, or mebby I'll go back over the trail with some bull train. There's talk of takin' over all of Mexico, an'. . . ."

"Stop it . . . stop it!" the girl cried out, her voice rising frenziedly. "Blood! Fighting! Drinking! Is that all life will ever mean to you?"

After a moment Rust spoke harshly. "Mebbe I been too busy livin' to think about life."

They plodded on in silence. Rust did not understand this girl. She was more of a mystery to him than that night back on the Missouri when he had first laid eyes on her as he stood on the prow of the *James Madison*. He was remembering the tenderness and devotion with which she had nursed Lee Fitzpatrick back to life there in the hidden camp on Raft River after the Shoshone fight. And he was recalling the affection she always displayed toward Rhoades and Swan and Magoffin.

Rust, marching side-by-side with the five of them, had never been one of them. He had been only a bystander, watching their close-knit relationship, but as remote from them as a shadow.

As he plodded with her through Carson Sink, he dully wondered if it was Rhoades she loved. The young doctor likely would make a name for himself in the future — if he lived. Rhoades was fully fitted to give a high-bred gentlewoman like Sue Hatfield the protection that was her right.

But there was Fitzpatrick, with his flashing ways, and big Toby Swan, who she had impulsively kissed more than once. And Rust remembered the high laughter in her eyes as she had danced with Waldo Magoffin to the *tinkle* of the banjo in camps on the far back trail. . . .

An ox failed toward midnight. Rust's gun sounded again, and they lurched on. Clyde Rhoades was beginning to stumble. Even big Swan's strength was failing.

Dawn lay beneath the black horizon. The story was nearly told. Another day in the sun would leave them here.

Then Rust lifted his head, sensing a quickening in the shambling gait of the cattle. He had his arm around Sue Hatfield, for she was walking in a half stupor.

"Water!" he croaked. "Grass! The critters smell it. We're nigh the meadows."

The dim line of cottonwoods came reluctantly out of the gray dawn ahead, and they heard the rush of clear water!

VIII

They were forced to spend a precious week, recruiting their strength, in the Truckee Meadows there in the shadow of the great Sierras. Southbound ducks and geese fell to the shotgun in the tule swamps; rabbits were plentiful. The five men and the girl recuperated on that fare and the oxen put on flesh.

Rust concealed his impatience. Each dawn he appraised the high mountains, praying for that first light blanket of snow to vanish. But it was still there in the late October sunlight when they broke camp.

"We'll leave the wagon," he stated casually, "an' carry packs. We'll drive the cattle with us. We'll siwash it over the hump, an' live on ox-steaks if need be."

He had read the portents. The ducks were southing early. The red squirrel and bobcat were wearing the heaviest coats he had ever seen, and deer were moving out of the high mountains.

They entered the mountains by way of a long cañon, with a rushing river in its depths. The desert sage and greasewood gradually gave way to pine and cedar, and the nights began to bite.

It was the route the Donner party had taken a few years before. But Rust did not mention that. On the fourth day, with the summit still remote, Rust watched gray clouds gather over the rims and creep out to enfold the sky. Dry snow began to sting their faces in the afternoon.

He chose a great granite boulder, adjacent to a pine forest. "Weather workin' up," he told them. "We'll camp here."

Rust and Swan built a snow-break for the cattle among the scrub pine, a dozen rods beyond the boulder. The wind increased steadily, driving snow in a blinding wall, and they had to fight their way back to the camp.

Sue was cooking the last of the dried rabbit meat they had brought in their packs. As the wind swooped under the wagon sheet that had been stretched as a roof, smoke stung her eyes. She searched Rust's face anxiously as he came into the cramped camp space and squatted to spread his hands over the blaze. With a shock, she realized how much he had changed. Somewhere on the Humboldt Desert, he had abandoned his ragged buckskin for wool and linsey garb that he had salvaged from an abandoned wagon. His clothes hung loosely on his gaunt frame. His weathered skin was drawn tightly over his cheek bones.

Clyde Rhoades saw Sue studying the mountain man, and read her thoughts. He lifted his eyes to Rust, appraising him.

"Rust," he spoke slowly, "you've done the work of three

men on the trail, and now, that I think back over it, I recall that you never uttered a complaint. At times I've looked down on you. Sometimes I almost hated you. But a man lives and learns. No matter what happens, I hope that you and I will never be far apart again."

Rust looked at him, a queer glint in his eyes. "Yeah, Rhoades," he said. "A man does learn, don't he?"

A stiff restraint fell upon them all, but it seemed to Zeke Rust that he was now one of them. He was no longer a shadow.

The darkness came prematurely, the wind cannonading down the ridges and churning the forest to a roaring sea. Snow spat in the fire and swept over their shelter in a moaning, dizzy wall.

Fitzpatrick spread the blankets, and they turned in. Rust kept replenishing the fire as the night advanced, but the chill mountain storm became a sharp-toothed force, hour by hour.

Sue Hatfield muttered in her blankets. Once she screamed out: "Rust! Quick! The tomahawk!"

She partly awakened, and saw Rust stretched out beside her. Like a child, she crept nearer him, pillowing her head on his shoulder. And there she slept.

Magoffin was awake. He lay a long time watching Sue, and something akin to hopeless acceptance dulled his face. He saw to the fueling of the fire for the rest of the night, so that Rust could sleep without disturbing the exhausted girl.

At dawn the violence of the blizzard was that of a released demon having his fling. There were no mountains, no sky, no earth. Snow and a primitive wind possessed the world.

Sue awakened and found Rust's eyes close at hand, looking gravely into her own. She smiled a little. Then, fully arousing, she sat up suddenly. A stain of color worked into the wan depths of her face. Her glance turned swiftly to the other four men, and something like wondering dismay showed in her eyes.

Rust arose, looked grimly out at the storm. Then he picked up an axe and a skinning knife. His lips were wry. Oxen were dumb brutes, but those five survivors of the teams had gone through the same hardships and suffering as their drivers.

Toby Swan's big hands took the edged implements from Rust. "Damn it, Rust, we ain't babies," he complained. "I'll do this job."

Swan pushed his great shoulders beyond the windbreak into the wall of the blizzard. He was gone from sight and sound instantly.

Rust made the cook fire ready and placed the camp in order with a restless energy. Then they waited for Swan to return.

Rust began to listen to the storm. He was beginning to wonder at Swan's overlong absence. At last he set his ragged hat low, tied it under his chin with a bandanna, and went out into the blizzard. Sue stood up as though to stop him, then thought better of it. There was a gray, dreadful apprehension in her silence.

The oxen had been picketed behind the snow break among the young pines. Rust had to dig in his toes and cling to branches as he quartered against the wind along the mountain slope. But there were no oxen among the trees. Rust picked up an ice-stiffened length of picket line, kicked in the snow, and found another. The animals had broken free and drifted with the storm!

He knelt and marked out the tracks of Toby Swan, already beginning to vanish under the steady beat of new snow.

Rust lifted his voice in an appalled shout: "Swan!"

The blizzard threw it back at him.

IX

Swan's tracks showed that he had gone down the mountain in pursuit of the cattle.

"The fool!" Rust groaned. "The brave, damned, sod-bustin' fool! He ain't got a chance." Then he remembered that none of them had a chance if Swan failed. The oxen were their only hope. And he understood completely why Swan had gone down alone on the trail.

Rust heard Sue's voice come swiftly down the channels of the wind. "Rust! Rust! Toby Swan!"

Rust did not answer. He set himself down the wind-beaten slope, following those dimming indentations made by Toby Swan's great boots. He paused every few strides to look back, to map in his mind the dim skyline of trees and the glimpses of white ridges and ledges that peered out from the blizzard.

The trail turned along a sandstone ledge that overlooked a great cañon, whose depths vanished in the spume of driving snow. He lost Swan's tracks on wind-polished granite beyond. And he could not find them again.

Rust fought the imponderable drifts and the muscle-cramping slants for what was an age to him. He sank down at last in the lee of a boulder, tasting the salt blood in his throat, his lungs sobbing. Zeke Rust had never before admitted defeat, but now it had come to him at a time, when above all others, he wanted to win.

Presently he began fighting his way back up the mountain in the face of the storm. More than once he paused, considered turning back. Toby Swan was down there somewhere giving his life in the hope of saving his comrades. . . .

But the need of the living lashed him to mount that ascent. Four of them were still alive up there, and somehow he might be able to get them through.

He was crawling, dragging himself ahead in laborious surges, with red froth on his lips, when Magoffin and Rhoades found him ten feet from the camp. They carried him in to the fire. Sue treated his frostbitten face and feet with snow.

He sat up and stared into the fire with dull eyes. Sue was kneeling near him.

"Toby?" she asked softly, and the tragic tenderness in her tone was like a benediction.

Rust did not lift his eyes. "The cattle had broke away and drifted with the storm. He followed 'em, knowin' that we needed 'em to live. I couldn't find him down there." He arose convulsively, in mad protest. "Why wasn't it me? He didn't know the mountains nor the ways of a blizzard. Why did I let him go? Why did I?"

Waldo Magoffin put his hands on Rust's shoulders. "Easy, Rust," he said gently. "Toby wouldn't have asked a better way to pass . . . fighting to save Sue and you and the rest of us. None of us would ask anything more than to die that way."

The blizzard, consumed by its own fury, died during the second night. The snow pack choked the timber and filled the small gulches. The mountains were impassable until the snow crusted.

Rust, his belt pulled to the last notch, stood staring down into the white depths of the great cañon from which Toby Swan would never return. She stood with him, thin, worn with starvation darkening her eyes.

148

Then Fitzpatrick touched his arm. "Rust!" he gritted hoarsely. "Look!"

A moving speck of grizzled brown showed against the fleecy glare of the new snow on a mountainside more than four hundred yards away. It was a buck deer!

Fitzpatrick hurriedly brought a rifle from the camp. There was a moment of hesitation, then he handed it to Rust.

Rust measured a fresh charge of powder in his palm, poured it, tamped a bullet down. The buck was struggling in heavy snow, making its way up the mountain. Rust looked at Sue Hatfield as he raised the gun. He loved her. He had come to admit that weeks ago, but he had kept the secret deep in his heart. Toby Swan had loved her, too, and had given his life.

As he laid the long barrel across a limb as a rest, he was conscious of the careless indifference of Lee Fitzpatrick, who stood near, without fear or concern on his reckless face. Rust was remembering that bloody dawn when Fitzpatrick had taken the tomahawk that was intended for him. And there were Rhoades and Magoffin, and he thought of the flooding Platte and the mocking aridity of the Carson Sink.

Zeke Rust had all of that on his mind as he laid the sights of the Sharps on that distant, lurching speck. If he brought down that deer, they still had a chance to live. If he missed. . . .

As he stood there motionless, the buck moved, fighting the drifts. The gun's brief report suddenly clattered. The deer turned and gave a great frightened bound. Then it headed up the mountainside, seeking cover in the timber.

Age seemed to leap upon Zeke Rust. He lowered the gun with trembling hands. "Missed!" he said, and his remorse was a terrible thing to hear. "I failed yuh. It's me that you'll curse as yuh starve."

Fitzpatrick caught his arm with fierce impatience. "You'd

think that of us, after what we've been through together?" he gritted. "Rust, we'd have been dead weeks ago but for you. That was an impossible shot. No livin' man could have made it in that sun-glare, under these condi. . . ."

"The deer!" Sue screamed. "Look!"

The buck's knees had caved. It staggered, fell, and rolled a dozen rods back down in the snow slant, then lay still.

When they reached it, they found that Rust's bullet had drilled it through.

The venison gave them strength to climb the pass after that crust hardened. Alder Creek and Donner Lake, where men and women had starved and died, lay silent under the snow as the four gaunt men and the hollow-eyed girl plodded by.

Two days' journey beyond the pass, Rust stopped and pointed. Ahead, cradled in a gulch, were cabins and the more pretentious structures of stores. Smoke came from chimneys.

"Illinoistown," Rust said hoarsely. "We've reached the Californy mines."

He turned and looked back at the mountains over which they had come, but Sue Hatfield grasped his arm fiercely.

"Don't look back, Rust," she said brokenly. "It's Toby you're thinking of. He wouldn't want it. Ahead is your life."

Her brown eyes were soft and pleading. Suddenly her arms went around his neck, drawing his head down to her face, and she kissed him. Then she began sobbing, clinging to him.

Rust had the eyes of a lost, bewildered man as he looked up at the other three.

Clyde Rhoades smiled, and did not show the hurt in his heart. "It's you, Rust," he said gruffly. "She's your life . . . your future. Don't you understand?"

Numbly Rust turned to Fitzpatrick and Magoffin. The fatalistic acceptance of luck ran in Fitzpatrick's thin face. "It's been you for weeks, Rust." He nodded. "None of us has been in her heart for a long time. You are the man."

Zeke Rust's arms tightened around the girl. "I ain't fit for her," he breathed. "But I love her."

A massive monument of native granite stands overlooking a great cañon on the east slope of the Sierras. Toby Swan's name is carved on it, together with the dates of his birth and death. Beneath is the epitaph: GREATER LOVE HATH NO MAN.

Each year in July, when the mountains are in bloom, a file of riders comes with pack animals to camp in dreamy peace near the monument.

There is the well-known physician from San Francisco, Dr. Clyde Rhoades, distinguished and aristocratic and the most sought-after bachelor in Nob Hill society. From Sacramento comes the wealthy merchant, Waldo Magoffin, with his pretty Spanish wife and their three husky children. And Lee Fitzpatrick, soldier and trail blazer, who is the husband of a talented and beautiful actress, never fails to be on hand.

The leader of the party is a tall, bronzed cattleman, whose *rancho* in the San Joaquin Valley of California is famous for its hospitality and for the beauty of the brown-eyed mistress. They always bring their lanky, sandy-haired son and a winsome daughter with sloe-brown eyes.

Occasionally the lean, weather-browned *ranchero* lapses into the dialect of the mountain men when yarning of the past. At such times the doctor and the prosperous merchant and the soldier lean back and listen. Their minds drift over the years. Vividly they see again Zeke Rust in his shrunken buckskins and with his wild grin, whacking bulls as the wagons rolled out from the Missouri River to meet the challenge of the great trail.

Then Zeke remembers, too, and grows silent as he looks up at the monument. He still does not understand why Toby Swan was the one marked to die.

No Peace for the Living

"No Peace for the Living" was completed in November, 1936 and sold to Popular Publications' *Ace-High Magazine*, where it appeared as the lead story in the issue dated April 1937, under the title "The Gringo Hell Let Loose". The latter title refers to the protagonist, a thrill-seeking young outlaw who must play a dangerous and life-changing game on both sides of the Río Grande in an effort to obtain his brother's release from prison. As in "Sign of the White Feather" and many other Farrell stories, the shadow of a long-standing feud raises major obstacles.

Blaze Cardwell had never before known that he possessed nerves. With a start, he discovered that he was riding with his six-shooter palmed, his thumb hard on the hammer. He had not remembered drawing the gun. It was not the first time in the past hour that he had found himself wire-taut in the saddle, crouching and scanning the shadows as though in expectancy of a sudden onrush of danger. He impatiently leathered the gun.

There was nothing amiss. He could see his swing and flank riders dimly through the moonlight. The three back in the drag were doing their work.

The sullen roar of hoofs went on monotonously as the dozen case-hardened border runners held them at a steady trot toward the ford of the Río Grande, now only half an hour's drive ahead. The cattle were thirsty. They were picking up the muddy, fishy scent of the river, and needed little hazing.

The night was hot and sultry. Heat lightning flickered far to the west, lifting the somber rims of the Sierra Del Burros into fitful silhouette. Overhead a half moon played tag with scattered clouds. A thin ground mist was rising from the river bosques and swamps.

It was a night made to order for running the river — with moonlight enough to handle the cattle, but with this low-lying mist to hamper watchful border guards or *rurales*. There was no sign of danger. Before dawn, the herd should be corralled in a hide-out on the Texas side that the border patrols had never stumbled upon.

Still that tension persisted in Blaze Cardwell's brawny, wide-shouldered body. He glanced back at a raw-boned, lank cowboy who was riding right point. Blaze's granite gray eyes softened a little. There, he told himself, was the reason for his apprehension.

The drive was following a shallow swale between brush-clad hills. The swale narrowed into a funnel gap ahead, up which poured the dank promise of the river. There was no need to pilot the herd here, so Blaze dropped back and rode at the side of the taller man.

"Easy pickings, Ran," he observed. "An' it pays a lot better than forty a month."

They were brothers. Ran Cardwell was in his early thirties, some six or seven years older than the flame-haired gun boss of the border runners. He was moody, with dark, serious eyes, and a certain tired droop in his shoulders. He looked as though life had treated him none too well. He was drab and colorless compared to his rugged, self-assured younger brother.

"It looks easy this far," Ran conceded. "Wet cattle pay better than punching jobs. But sometimes you get paid off in hot lead. Ever think of that, Tom?"

"Sounds good to hear you call me by my right handle." Blaze grinned. "Don't get in a sweat, worryin' about the hot lead. You'll shed that spooky feelin' in time. After all, this is your first border jump. You've got to take chances to make money, Ran."

"I've tried 'most everything else," Ran admitted. "I punched cows, an' always ended up with nothin' but a slick saddle an' empty poke. I tried runnin' my own brand, an' was stomped out by the big outfits. I dry farmed up in the territory, an' the grasshoppers ate me up. Maybe I'll have better luck at this sort of thing."

"I got you into this," Blaze stated, and there was a little, betraying hum of emotion in his throat. "I'll see that you get through safe. You've earned some luck, Ran."

Even while he talked to his brother, Blaze was watching the shadowy mesquite and scrub oak that drew in closer as the swale narrowed. He was thinking remotely that it would be pure, cruel hell if anything happened to Ran on his first ride.

Ran had never been cut out for this sort of thing. He had none of Blaze's wild, reckless blood. The zest for danger that bubbled in Blaze like exhilarating wine did not touch Ran's imagination. Blaze knew Ran was depressed and half ashamed of being here with these law-dodging cattle runners. To Blaze, this was a sport rather than a business. It was the accomplishment, rather than the profits, that appealed to him.

Right now, with the uneasy sense of unseen peril riding him, Blaze was vividly alive, with the blood singing a wild refrain in his arteries. Blaze Cardwell, red-headed, roistering fighting man, knew in his heart that he loved danger for danger's sake. Once this herd was delivered, the zest would be gone. That, no doubt, was the reason the money he derived never stayed long in his pockets.

"Who buys these wet steers?" Ran, always practical, wanted to know.

"A dealer in Laredo pays off." Blaze shrugged. "He acts for a cowman up in the Big Bend . . . name of Travis Merchant, though I'm not supposed to know that. I never met this Travis Merchant. No need to."

Ran stared at him. "Travis Merchant?" he echoed. "You ain't kiddin' me, are you, Tom? Why he's augur of a million-dollar outfit. His Rafter M covers plenty of range. They wanted Merchant to run for governor a few years ago. He ain't the kind to handle wet. . . ."

"Folks down here on the border look at wet ones different than you, maybe," said Blaze. "Ranchers like Merchant figure they're only gettin' back what has been stole from them in the past an' run the other way across the river. Plenty of border cowmen with reps for square-dealin' take on wet cattle, if the price is right."

"I wouldn't believe it," Ran muttered. "I peeled bronc's at the Rafter M a few years back. Merchant is. . . ."

Without warning, like a savage tidal wave, a swarm of yelling horsemen erupted from the chaparral on the right. In the dim moonlight, Blaze saw crossed bandoliers and steeple-crowned hats shadowing swarthy faces.

"¡Rurales!" he yelled. "Ride! We're in a trap."

Blaze's words were inaudible even to his own ears, lost in the tumult. The herd was stampeding. Fifty carbines were throwing lead. The reports of the guns snapped like the clicking teeth of wolves through the roar of hoofs as the cattle hit full, panicky stride.

"This way!" Blaze bellowed frantically at his brother. "Straight ahead! Down the draw! The river's your only chance."

But Ran could not hear. Inexperienced in the ways of the danger trails, he lacked his brother's ability to meet a crisis like this. Maddened cattle swept between them, separating them. Dust swirled up, engulfing the scene.

Blaze caught a glimpse of Ran, riding blindly across the point of the stampede, racing for the silent, dark wall of chaparral on the opposite side of the draw from which the *rurales* had appeared.

"Ran!" Blaze shouted. "No! Straight ahead! Ride it out! There'll be more of 'em there to. . . ."

A bullet drilled Blaze's mount. The horse staggered, then pitched in a somersault. Blaze hurled his body clear, landed on hands and knees. A stampeding steer brushed him and sent him staggering. For an instant he was caught in a surge of running steers. He escaped that danger. Somehow he managed to race clear of the maëlstrom of yelling, shooting *rurales,* and berserk cattle. He had his six-shooter in his hand, but had not yet fired a shot. He glimpsed some of his men. Their guns were flaming.

Two of his riders saw him and veered to pick him up. Bullets smashed them from the saddle before they reached him. One riderless horse came on, careening crazily through the press of men and horses. Blaze caught the saddle horn and leaped astride as the animal passed at a frenzied lope.

The curtain of dust and the river mists shielded him. He rode clear of the dust, whirled his horse. A groan of sheer agony came from his lips. Four of his border hoppers, who had escaped the first onslaught, were riding for the brush to the left. Ran was one of them.

Blaze stood up in the stirrups, his teeth clenched. He sensed what was coming. He averted his eyes as he saw the opposite line of brush erupt a new wave of *rurales*. Rifles flamed savagely; Blaze could hear the reports faintly through the roar of the stampede. When Blaze looked again, the four American border runners were no longer riding. Three horses were down; the fourth, wounded and riderless, staggered in circles.

It was over! Blaze turned his mount and headed down the draw. As his escape was discovered, bullets snapped around him, tugging at his woolen shirt and brush-scarred chaps.

He could hear the *rurales* thundering in pursuit as he raced through the narrow mouth of the draw and emerged into the open, marshy bosques along the river. The mists were heavier here, with an eerie dankness. He abandoned his horse in the thickets, floundered on foot through mud and reedy swamps. Here, horsemen could not follow.

Four days later, alone, Blaze rode into Esteros, a little adobe-and-mud outlaw rendezvous, deep in the mesquitals on the American side of the Río Grande. He was haggard and hollow-eyed, and there was black remorse in his eyes.

In Tomás Sanchez's *cantina*, Blaze found one of the twelve who had been with him that night. He was a tough slit-eyed veteran of the outlaw trails named Woody Searles.

"I slipped away in the fog," Woody said moodily. "I figgered I was the only one. I heard you had gone under, Blaze. I reckon they must have mistaken Red Stiles for you. His hair was as red as yours."

They downed a drink in silence.

"Damned near a wipe out," Woody muttered. "We left

seven good boys back there with their toes curled up. At that, maybe they're luckier'n your brother an' Kaw Devers an' Spoke Jessup."

Blaze straightened. "What do you mean?"

Woody was startled by the expression on the brawny red-head's unshaven face. "Didn't yuh hear?" he stammered. "Your brother was took alive, along with Spoke an' Kaw."

"Firin' squad?" Blaze asked hoarsely.

Woody shook his head grimly. "Nothin' as easy as that. They was given a drum-head trial at Cabazón the next day. They got life sentences in El Citadel. That's the Mex prison the *peónes* call the *casa del diablo* . . . House of the Devil. Life, hell! No *gringo* lives long there. It only seems long."

Icy sweat came slowly out on Blaze Cardwell's freckled forehead. He sat there with big fists knotted, looking at nothing. The remorse in his eyes deepened into black hopelessness. The things Blaze had heard about El Citadel, the bleak stone prison on the bluff overlooking Cabazón, ran fearfully through his mind.

"I talked Ran into riding with me," he muttered, talking only to himself. "I promised nothing would happen to him. Now he's rotting away in El Citadel." He put down his empty glass, and arose.

"Where you goin', Blaze?" Woody Searles asked quickly.

"To Cabazón."

Woody shrugged. "It's no use. They say nobody ever escaped from that rathole in the bluff. Bribery might git 'em out, but the price is high. Ramón Morales is *comandante* there. He can't be bought for a song."

"I'll get him out of there," Blaze stated flatly. "I got 'im into that place. It's up to me."

Woody Searles watched him go out into the darkness. "Damn' glad he didn't ask me to go with him," Woody told

Tomás Sanchez, the fat barkeeper. "It ain't healthy to say
'No' to Blaze Cardwell when his eyes go cold an' flat like
that. . . . It don't take long fer the buzzards to pick your bones
clean in that mesquite desert around Cabazón. He'll make a
good-lookin' skeleton, Tomás. Let's have another bottle of
mescal."

II

"TOMB OF THE LIVING DEAD"

The adobe walls and wattled roofs of Cabazón straggled in
the shadow of the frowning prison on the bluff. Situated some
eighty miles south of the river, in a sand-colored mesquite
plain between low, outflung arms of the Burro Range, the
town catered to the prison hill garrison and to the spike-
heeled, leather-mailed *vaqueros* from the big *ranchos* that nes-
tled in the mountains.

Cabazón paid only passing attention to the arrival from
the north of the *gringo* rider whose hair was as red as the
desert sunset. For the dusty, crowded town was host, that
evening, to other — and more celebrated — *gringo* visitors.

It was the eve of the Feast of San Juan. The great white-
walled *casa* of *El Coronel* Ramón Morales, set in a niche on the
side of the bluff above the village, was ablaze with lights. In
the walled enclosure were the carriages and saddle mounts of
the most important *hacendados* and *políticos* of the region as
well as of American dignitaries from beyond the Río Grande.

After Blaze Cardwell had put up his horse, he stood for a
time grimly eyeing the squat outline of the great stone prison
on the lip of the bluff. El Citadel crouched against the bright,

pinpoint canopy of stars like a gigantic toad, looking down on the village with blank, slitted eyes that were heavily barred windows. Half a thousand hopeless men were entombed behind those heavy, gray walls. . . . Men without hope!

Blaze felt the menace and mocking power of the prison. He sensed his own impotence against its massive strength. A sick feeling came to the pit of his stomach as he pictured Ran up there with the rats and vermin that were said to make sleep worse than a fevered nightmare.

A religious procession pushed through the crowded street, with *ocotillo* torches flaring. There was music, dancing, and drinking in the *cantinas*. *Vaqueros* were vying at chicken pulling and wild horse riding in the fire-lighted plaza. And the solemn bell in the old church kept tolling the call to the faithful. Gaiety and piety walked side-by-side in Cabazón that night.

Blaze wet his throat with *aguardiente* in a *cantina*. As he walked with the crowd, his eyes kept straying to that tomb of living men up there in the starlight. He listened to the talk around, but heard no word that would help him.

He looked up, aroused by a *clatter* of hoofs. The crowd was parting hastily, clearing the narrow roadway. *Peónes* were sweeping off their *jipi* hats and bowing low.

Half-hearted approbation arose. "*¡Viva el coronel! ¡Vaya con Dios!* Go with God!"

A big, glittering carriage, with four spirited bays in the harness, came racing through the lanes of humanity. Blaze pressed back to make room, growling at the recklessness of the uniformed driver.

A woman's frightened scream shrilled over the hubbub. Blaze turned. With a cry of dismay, he saw a little brown-faced child run in glee from his mother — directly into the path of the oncoming carriage.

161

The *soldado* handling the reins did not see the *niño*. And the horses, maddened by the crowd and flaring torches, were at almost a full gallop.

The lead team was plunging abreast of Blaze. He did the only thing possible. With a violent drive of his muscles, he leaped, caught the bit chains, and threw the horses off stride. The animals reared, lifting him and veered violently into the opposite line of spectators, where *vaqueros* and *soldados* halted them.

The carriage wheels cramped; the vehicle came within an ace of capsizing. It settled back with a jerk. Blaze turned, grinning faintly as he saw the Mexican mother gather up the child and vanish in the crowd. He released the horses and stepped back.

An elegant figure in the gold-decked uniform of a Mexican colonel stood up in the carriage, glaring at the red-haired *gringo*. "What is the meaning of this, fool?" he demanded harshly in Spanish.

A clear, feminine voice spoke up quickly in English. "Wait, uncle! There was a *niño* in the way. The man stopped the carriage just in time. I saw the child, but was too horrified to shout at the driver in time."

Blaze saw that there were four more passengers in the carriage with the colonel. In the glare of torches he noticed that one was a spare, stern-faced American, who had "cattleman" stamped indelibly on him. Beside him was a *mantilla*-clad *señora* and a younger, fair-haired girl.

He noted these three absently, for his gaze was fixed with surprise on the girl who had risen to her feet to admonish the arrogant officer. Big, liquid dark eyes smiled down at Blaze, from a proud, oval face, faintly olive-tinted. A little garland of flowers held down the mass of her hair, which glinted raven-black in the flickering light. Accented cheek bones and

162

curving, red lips showed her Spanish strain. But her speech, her garb, and her manner told Blaze that here was a girl who was an American by birth and training and instinct.

Blaze removed his dusty hat. "I'm sorry I startled you, *señorita*," he said. "I had to act in a hurry."

Her smile flashed brighter. "I knew you were a Texas cowboy the instant I saw you leap at the horses," she said, and he could see the elusive dimple that played in her cheek. "I was frightened out of a year's growth, I want you to know."

The gold-braided officer shrugged. He snapped a curt order, and the bystanders freed the quieted horses.

"This will repay you for your trouble," the colonel said coldly in perfect English.

He tossed a gold coin as the carriage leaped away. Blaze caught it. He saw the dark-haired girl looking back at him. With a laugh, he flipped the gold piece into the crowd, and watched the wild scramble.

"And who was the great one?" he asked a *soldado*.

"Ah, *señor,* you are indeed a stranger in Cabazón. It was none other than *El Coronel* Ramon Morales, *comandante* of El Citadel. And with him was his brother-in-law, the rich *americano, Señor* Merchant, who is said to possess uncounted leagues of land and thousands of. . . ."

Blaze's eyes went hard and bright. "*Señor* Merchant?" he interrupted. "Did I hear you correct, *amigo?*"

"To be sure. The *Señor* Travis Merchant comes each year with his *duena* and his beautiful *doncellitas* to pass the Feast of San Juan at the *casa*. This is indeed your lucky night. I would give much to have done such service for the great ones, and to have received the smile from the beautiful *Señorita* Consuelo Merchant."

Blaze stood staring at the garrulous soldier, without seeing him. His eyes had gone hard and reflective. "Maybe you're right, *amigo*," he muttered. "Maybe this is my lucky night."

Blaze moved away through the crowd. Cold fury began to surge in him. Blaze was thinking of the trap into which he and his riders had fallen that night nearly two weeks before. That trap had not been a matter of accident. Someone had sent information to the *rurales*.

Blaze had placed the blame on the slippery, wet cattle dealer in Laredo. He had visited Laredo, intending to wring the truth from the man. But his quarry had disappeared.

He stood there, staring grimly up at the brightly lighted *casa*. It was *El Coronel* Morales, as military *comandante* of this district, who had received credit for wiping out those bold, *gringo* cattle runners that night. That exploit had strengthened the prestige of Morales and earned him congratulations from Mexico City.

Blaze pieced the facts together. Morales was Travis Merchant's brother-in-law, and Travis Merchant had been a heavy buyer of wet cattle. Most of the steers Blaze and his men had run across the river had gone eventually to Merchant's big ranch up in the Big Bend.

Travis Merchant probably knows how and why the rurales *came to be hunkered there, waiting for us, that night,* Blaze thought, and his lips were a hard, straight line. *He likely had decided to quit buying wet cattle, and wanted to wipe out his back trail. And in cleaning his own skirts he was able to do a favor for his brother-in-law.*

Then he thought of the pretty, dark-haired girl — the daughter of Travis Merchant. Some of his bitter triumph died. But his purpose remained unchanged.

Travis Merchant's visit at the *casa* lasted more than a week. Blaze glimpsed him occasionally, whirling away on

164

horseback or by carriage to pay his respects to some of the *hacendados* of the surrounding range. Always he was accompanied by the *comandante* and escorted by a saber-jingling troop of cavalry.

Blaze scouted the *casa* at night, but found it too well guarded to attempt an entrance. He bided his time. He wanted to confront Travis Merchant alone, without danger of interruption.

He saw Merchant's daughters several times in the village, always escorted by a retinue of enamored young officers from the garrison. He had learned that the younger, fair-haired daughter was named Amata. She looked to be about nineteen. Her sister was a year or two older.

Consuelo, with her dark hair and flashing black eyes, saw him once on the street in Cabazón. Her smile of recognition was friendly. Blaze lifted his hat with cool formality. He tried afterward to forget the loveliness of Consuelo Merchant.

Blaze stood in a *cantina* door, his hat low over his eyes, the morning Travis Merchant and his family whirled out of Cabazón, their visit concluded. An escort of cavalry rode with the carriage up the trail to the river.

That afternoon Blaze also headed north, back to Texas soil. He looked back at El Citadel on the bluff.

"I'll come back, Ran," he said aloud.

III

"BIG BEND GUN KING"

A week later, in the sultry, early darkness of a summer night, Blaze dismounted at a distance from the scattered lights that marked the Rafter M headquarters. He tied his horse to a mesquite, moved slowly in on foot.

Travis Merchant's ranch had the character of an ancient stronghold. There was all the evidence of rude, feudal power in the scatter of buildings. A village of more than a score of adobe houses, for the *peónes* and field workers, stood on the flat. There were stores and storehouses, thick-walled granaries and wagon sheds, blacksmith shops where large forge fires still flickered and anvils *clanged*.

The fragrance of irrigated alfalfa and tilled fields rode the night breeze. About the spread was the comfortable, drowsy stir of humans relaxing from the day's activities.

The ranch house stood apart on a small knoll, shadowed by ancient cottonwoods and sycamores. Adobe-built, with tile roofs, its white-washed walls formed a solid, massive pattern in the starlight as Blaze approached. A fountain gurgled in the flower-scented patio, and from one of the softly lighted windows drifted the vagrant *tinkle* of a piano.

Blaze had his hand on the grip of his gun as he reached the patio, but he entered unchallenged. The curtains stood open in the deep-set windows. He looked into the window through which the music came. And then he regretted that he had looked.

Consuelo Merchant sat at a big, square piano, running her fingers dreamily over the keys in the melody of some old Spanish love song. A simple, short-sleeved gingham frock covered the symmetry of her figure.

Amata, the golden-haired one, slim and young, and delicately beautiful, stood beside the piano, thumbing through a pile of sheet music. And the girls' mother, a sweet-faced, aristocratic woman of magnetic dark-haired beauty, sat quietly knitting in the glow of a brass-bowled table lamp.

Blaze turned his eyes away from that window with an effort. His glance swung to the opposite wing of the rambling house. Through another window he looked into a more severe room, adorned with saddles and the guns and gear of an active man of the open.

Travis Merchant, in plain cotton shirt, Levi's, and boots, with steel-rimmed spectacles on his hawk-like nose, sat at a desk, working on the ranch books.

Blaze tiptoed to the window and made sure that Merchant was alone. There was a door leading into the room adjoining the rancher's private den. Blaze stepped without a sound into the house. He moved through the half opened door into the owner's den. His spurs rang softly, causing Travis Merchant to look up.

Merchant put down the pen, measuring Blaze with curt inquiry. "What do you want?" he snapped. His harsh eyes, set deeply beneath thin, graying brows, matched the stony gray bluntness of Blaze's gaze.

Blaze crossed to the window. He drew the heavy drapes. "You don't know me, eh, Merchant?" he asked, a mocking rasp in his voice.

Merchant's gun belt hung on a peg across the room. His glance flickered briefly to it, but the gun was out of quick reach.

"What's on your mind?" he demanded slowly. "How did you get in here?"

"Walked in. You take long chances, Merchant. When you double-cross a man, you ought to at least keep your house guarded."

Travis Merchant's lips curled in a scornful smile. "I never double-crossed a man in my life. Who are you?"

"Blaze Cardwell is the name. Maybe you've heard it before."

Merchant showed no surprise. Instead, he nodded. "At

least you tell the truth. I wondered if you'd admit your name. I've never had the doubtful pleasure of meeting you, but I have read your description on Cattle Association posters more than once, Cardwell. Your red hair brands you. But I had heard that you were dead. The newspapers say you and your border runners were wiped out down the river a few weeks ago."

"You know more about that slaughter than the newspapers told," Blaze stated coldly. "You laid that trap for us, Merchant. Seven of the boys died there that night. Three more are rotting in El Citadel."

Travis Merchant's head lifted in scornful pride. "You're loco or too drunk, Cardwell. I laid no trap for you or your outlaws. By what process of reasoning do you blame me?"

Blaze stood a moment, sizing him up. He had the feeling that he had never encountered a man with a will as steely and ruthless as this man's. There was no sign of weakness or fear in Travis Merchant.

"You were buying the cattle that we ran," Blaze said softly. "I learned that from Abe Miller in Laredo more than a year ago. He was your agent. You decided it was time to quit dealing with border hoppers, and clean your skirts. You sold us out to your brother-in-law, the *comandante* at El Citadel."

Travis Merchant sat frowning thoughtfully, pinning Blaze with unswerving eyes. "I savvy," he nodded musingly. "I follow your viewpoint. It's true I buy wet cattle . . . every border rancher does at times. An' Ramón Morales is my brother-in-law. He rods the *rurales* who salted you that night. But he didn't get the information from me. How could he? I knew nothin' about you, Cardwell. I dealt only with Abe Miller. You meant nothin' to me then, and you mean nothin' to me now."

"You're lyin', Merchant. It's no use. I came here to kill you."

Blaze was bluffing. The last thing he wanted was to have to kill Travis Merchant. Merchant, dead, could not free his brother from El Citadel. What Blaze sought was to drive some spark of fear into those scornful, bleak eyes, to break the contemptuous defiance on those thin, arrogant lips.

He failed completely. Travis Merchant sat there, looking at him with faint, bitter amusement.

"I've never crawled to any man, Cardwell," he said. "I'm too old to learn now. My gun is across the room. You've got things your own way. I've lived half a century. I'm not afraid to die."

Black bafflement beat at Blaze. He stood silently, considering his course.

Merchant leaned across the desk. "You're running a long bluff, Cardwell," he jeered. "If you really meant to rub me out, I'd have been dead by this time. You came here for something else. What is it?"

The pound of galloping hoofs silenced them. They heard the spurred boots of a fast-moving rider hit the ground and come striding into the patio.

Blaze glanced at Merchant, then, with a shrug, stepped back into the unlighted adjoining room. He moved out of sight behind the intervening door just before the rider burst in from the patio. The stranger strode past and into Merchant's office.

He was a weathered, saddle-warped oldster. His bowed bull-hide chaps rasped as he moved. As he strode into the lamplight, Blaze, through the opening back of the door, saw the deep, seething fury that worked in the man's lined, whiskery face.

Travis Merchant had come to his feet, and now stood within reach of his gun. For an instant the two glared at each

169

other in silence. Blaze saw the deadly antagonism between them.

The stocky cowman was breathing fast. "Belt on your gun, Merchant," he spat hoarsely. "Yuh laid a quirt across the face of my son in town today. Yuh said things to him that yuh've got to back up with powder smoke. He was too much of a man to take yuh to the cleanin' yuh deserved. He respected your age."

"He was too much of a yalla-livered sand crawler, you mean," Travis Merchant gritted, his voice shaking with surcharged emotion. "I called him a wigglin' side-windin' snake. I told him if he ever so much as even looked at my daughter again, I'd run him out of this range. He had the sneering impudence to say he wanted to marry Amata. I'd rather see her married to a Digger Injun than to the son of Joe Sealy."

"You've hated me for twenty-five years, Merchant," the old-timer said thickly. "An' I've despised you. Now you aim to turn your poison on my son. I'd rather see him dead than married to any of your blood and flesh. But there's no danger of that. He'll come to his senses in time. But for what you done to Steve there in Latigo today, I'm gut-shootin' you. . . . Hang on your cutter! I'll give yuh a chance to drag it. That's more'n you'd ever give me."

"You ratty old wolf!" Travis Merchant snarled, reaching for his gun belt. "I've let you live too long. We should have settled this twenty-five years ago."

Blaze stepped into the room, coming up behind Joe Sealy in a quick stride. He snatched the six-shooter from Sealy's holster. With a thrust of his arm, he pushed Sealy aside, then jerked the gun belt from Merchant's grasp.

"No killin' tonight, *amigos*," he said with a bleak grin. "Better cool off an' drag out of here, Sealy."

Joe Sealy glared at him with contempt. "Might have

170

known Travis Merchant would have some tough gunslick guardin' him, after what he did today," he spat. "Merchant ain't man enough to fight his own battles."

"Give us them guns," Merchant snarled at Blaze. "This old skunk has been askin' for it a long time."

Blaze heard a rush of skirts. He turned. Consuelo Merchant stood in the door, her eyes wide with apprehension. She stared from Joe Sealy to her father, and Blaze could see the fast hammer beat of her pulse quivering in her throat. Her gaze swung to him, and she straightened visibly with surprise as she recognized him.

"Father!" she breathed, and darted to Merchant, sliding her arms around his neck, and standing to shield him with her lithe, long-limbed body.

Blaze, with a stony expression, looked at Joe Sealy, and saw that the lightning had died from the old man's faded brown eyes. The arrival of the girl had ended all thought of gun play.

Blaze silently handed Sealy his gun. The sandy-whiskered cowman took it and stood an instant, with taut jaws. Then he strode from the house. His spurs rang briefly in the patio; a moment later the quick pound of hoofs told that Joe Sealy was leaving the Rafter M.

Consuelo spoke shakily to her father: "What happened?"

"The damned old fool came here to kill me," Merchant said curtly.

"Oh, Dad! Why can't you be friends? You and Joe Sealy have fought each other ever since I can remember. This can't go on. You've got to end this old feud. It's time both of you came to your senses."

"It'll be ended soon," her father declared with cold fury. "I laid a quirt on his whelp son today for havin' the impudence to ask if he could court Amata. I should have killed him."

"You didn't!" Consuelo protested frantically. "Oh, Dad! You didn't strike Steve Sealy! You don't know what you're doing. Why Amata and Steve. . . ."

She went silent as her father turned on her, a terrible glitter in his eyes. "What's that?" he gritted. "What about Amata? You don't mean to tell me she's been encouragin' Joe Sealy's rat-eyed son to make love to her?"

Consuelo straightened, and there was more than a trace of her father's iron will in her face. "Amata is nineteen. She knows her own heart, Dad," she said steadily. "Steve Sealy is an honest, hard-working young cowman. If they love each other, you can't let some old, secret grudge stand in the way of their happiness."

The veins stood out like rigid, blue bands on Merchant's temples. "So that's what Joe Sealy's son has been doin' behind my back," he breathed hoarsely. He sank into the chair at his desk. "Go back to your mother," he commanded shortly. "I'll join you there later. I've got a little more business to clean up."

The girl stood for a moment, looking from her father to Blaze. Blaze could see the apprehension that crowded her mind. But she said nothing. She walked from the room with that same, stiff pride that her father had displayed.

IV

"GUNFIGHTER'S PRICE"

Merchant sat staring at Blaze. At last he spoke. "For a man here to kill me, you failed to play your part, Cardwell. You had the chance to watch me die, an' no blame would have been on your head. Joe Sealy is greasy fast with a gun. He'd have killed me."

"I can't afford to let you die yet," Blaze remarked tersely. "You're worth more to me alive than dead. I don't want to kill you, nor do I want anybody else to rub you out, Merchant . . . not until I'm through with you."

"An' just what use am I to a border-hopping outlaw, Cardwell?"

"My brother was taken alive in your *rurale* trap," Blaze stated. "And two more good men . . . Kaw Devers an' Spoke Jessup. They're guests of your brother-in-law in El Citadel. Merchant, you're going to use your influence with the *comandante* to allow them to escape from that hell-hole."

Merchant shrugged. "It's none of my responsibility. I had no hand in that trap. Maybe that wet cattle dealer, Abe Miller, sold you out. I won't do a thing for your pals."

Blaze's wide jaws were like carved rock. "They're dying in El Citadel by inches . . . like you'll die, unless they're released, Merchant," he grated. "You're the only man who can free them. Now you savvy what you got to do?"

Merchant only laughed at him. "If I raised the long yell, fifty men would swarm down on you before you could spook away from this house, Cardwell," he warned.

It was Blaze's turn to smile mirthlessly. "If you raise your voice, I'll put a bullet down your gullet," he stated coolly. "You're not that anxious to die, Merchant."

Merchant leaned back in his chair, studying Blaze. "I owe you nothing, Cardwell," he said flatly. "But it might be that one good turn would deserve another. I could see to it that your pals escape from El Citadel . . . if I considered myself indebted to you."

"What are you driving at?" Blaze asked slowly.

Merchant lowered his voice. "I've thought of a little riding

173

job that a salty rannihan like you could do. You've had experience at it. I'd consider it a great favor."

"What sort of a riding job?"

"A matter of running new brands on a few white-faces that I own. . . . I reckon it wouldn't be the first time you've used a runnin' iron, Cardwell. There'd be no risk to it. The minute the job is finished to my satisfaction, your brother and these other two you mentioned will go free from El Citadel."

"I didn't come here to take on an owlhoot job for you, Merchant," Blaze snapped.

"You came here to haze me into freeing your pals. I won't be forced, Cardwell. You have my terms. Take 'em or get out."

Blaze was silent for a time, his face bleak. "You've got me hog-tied, Merchant," he admitted hoarsely. "I've never knuckled to any man before. But I've got to get those riders out of that *cuartel*. Let's hear your plan."

Merchant picked up a pen. He drew an insignia on a scrap of paper. "That's the Wishbone brand. I own it. Bought it from a busted outfit outside of Marfa a few months ago. I located the Wishbone herd, numbering about eleven hundred head, on my own summer range below Bowie Creek, about a dozen miles south of the ranch." He added a few pen marks to the brand. "That makes it an Hourglass. It's a cinch to run. I want you to move fifty or sixty head of Wishbone steers back into the hills, and work 'em over into the Hourglass iron. Then I'll tell you where to shove 'em."

"A man lives an' learns," Blaze said scornfully. "I never heard of an owner hiring brand blotters to work over his own stock. Who owns the Hourglass?"

"That's none of your worry, Cardwell."

"I can guess," Blaze snapped. "Joe Sealy, the old-timer

who aimed to ventilate you a few minutes ago. You aim to frame him as a rustler."

"He *is* a rustler. Him an' his slick son have stole cattle from me for years. I've never been able to get the deadwood on him."

Blaze's strong fingers hungered for the feel of Travis Merchant's throat. "I ought to rip you apart and see what kind of yellow poison would run from you," he breathed. "Do you think I'm skunk enough to help railroad a man to prison?"

"You're wrong there." Merchant shrugged, unmoved. "I'll see that the Sealys have their chance to run for it. All I want is for them to pull out of this range. They won't lose much. That Hourglass ranch is a shoe-string outfit."

"It's still skunk . . . from claws to hide," Blaze rasped. "Your price is too high, Merchant."

"They say an *americano* doesn't live long in El Citadel," Merchant murmured mockingly. "I'm surprised to hear that you have scruples, Cardwell. I understood differently. Listen to me. Joe Sealy's son is trying to steal my daughter. I happen to love Amata too dearly to see her waste her life on a man who is only hoping to marry her in order to make me suffer."

Blaze was torn between fury and futility. At last he laughed shortly, bitterly. "You've given your word that nobody will go over the road for this rotten scheme," he grated. "I don't figure a few blotted brands will stop a real man from taking the girl he loves. An' if he ain't a real man, there'll be no harm done, either. You've got me whipsawed. I'll do your dirty work, Merchant."

Merchant arose and went to a safe. He counted out some bills and tossed them to Blaze. "You'll need half a dozen men," he said. "There's half of what I'll pay them. I'll see that you have a clear trail. I'll pull out the two line riders from that

Wishbone range whenever you're ready. Where can I get in touch with you?"

"You'll hear from me inside a week," Blaze remarked. "In case you don't, you can get word to me in care of Tomás Sanchez, who runs the *cantina* in Esteros, down the river about eighty miles."

All the reckless, buoyant spirit was gone from Blaze as he turned to leave. He paused at the door. "If you double-cross me, Merchant," he stated slowly, "I'll break you inch by inch with my hands. You hear me?"

He went out, stumbling over the flagging in the patio with lifeless feet. Blaze was sick to his soul. He had followed the long trails with the thoughtless, hasty exuberance of a boy, ever hungry for excitement and adventure. Now the outlaw trail, for him, had taken a downward plunge into a slimy sink whose stain would never be erased from his soul.

He walked blindly out of the big ranch house into the clean, bright starlit night, heading toward his horse. A shadow moved in the deep gloom under the cottonwoods. Blaze stopped abruptly as Consuelo Merchant stepped out to confront him. Her face was a pale shadow in the light reflected from the ranch house windows.

"You are the *americano* who saved that *niño* from the hoofs of my uncle's carriage team in Cabazón," she murmured. "What are you doing here?"

Blaze shrugged. "I had business with your father, Miss Merchant. A cattle deal."

"This business," she said coldly, "does not concern Joe Sealy and the feud he has with my father, I trust? That can be settled without the help of Blaze Cardwell, the notorious border runner."

"So you know me."

"I recognized you that night in Cabazón. The El Paso and

Marfa papers carried long accounts of your death at the hands of my uncle's *rurales*. You and your wild exploits were well described. It was a nice epitaph for a cattle thief. Lucky for you that you were not so widely advertised in Mexico. Perhaps Colonel Morales would have recognized you, also, and realized that you were not dead after all."

"One of my *compañeros,* who was slaughtered by the *rurales,* had red hair," Blaze commented briefly. "His body was identified by the *rurales* as mine."

"If anything should happen to Joe Sealy or his son, the authorities might be interested to learn that Blaze Cardwell is still alive," she said. "Keep that in mind. I hope I won't see you talking in whispers to my father again. *¡Adiós!*"

She walked proudly away. Blaze watched her slim, lithe figure until the shadows of the patio had swallowed it. Then he went on and found his horse. He headed south toward Esteros, the outlaw rendezvous in the mesquitals.

V

"HANG ROPE FOR RUSTLERS"

Tomás Sanchez's dingy *cantina* in Esteros was filled with ghosts for Blaze. Black memories crowded his mind — memories of wild, carefree nights as he and his rash-tempered, hard-riding men rolled them high here, frittering away the profits of some dangerous sortie across the Río Grande.

Now seven of them were dead, their bullet-shattered bodies moldering in shallow, unmarked graves on the Mexican side of the river. Kaw Devers and Spoke Jessup were in El Citadel along with his brother. Even Woody Searles was gone. He had drifted away from Esteros. It was Tomás Sanchez's opinion that Woody had quit the long trails, and would be seen no more on the border.

In a way Blaze was glad none of them was here. He would have been ashamed to ask them to go in on the job he had agreed to do.

He spoke to Tomás. "Send word to Tony Slate that I'd like a palaver with him. I've got a job in mind that might be in his line."

It was not easy to surprise Tomás Sanchez, but now his fat, little face went blank. "Surely, *Señor* Blaze, you make the . . . what you call . . . ? You keed me. You do not mean to be seen talking to that *cabrón,* Tony Slate."

"It's a job that only buzzards would go for." Blaze shrugged. "Slate is the gent I want, if he hasn't been hung yet. An' I can use about four more of his rat-eyed bunch."

Tomás looked dubious, but sent a messenger. Within an hour a slovenly, unsavory outlaw, packing a brace of guns, swaggered in. He wore a greasy *charro* jacket, batwing chaps over ragged jeans, and broken, run-down Chihuahua boots.

Tony Slate was the type of border renegade who men like Blaze Cardwell despise and avoid like slinking, snarling curs. Slate had weasel-faced followers who would knife a man in the back for a few dollars. It was said that the gallows awaited Slate in more than one place in the West.

He approached Blaze doubtfully. "I sent for you, Slate," Blaze said curtly. "Come over to a table, an' I'll tell you what I want."

The conference did not last long. Blaze did all the talking, and he did not go into details. Tony Slate was only too glad to throw in with Blaze Cardwell; the alliance with the brawny, fighting redhead would give him standing.

But Blaze was keenly aware of the evil soul beneath the man's mask of fawning servility. Tony Slate had not forgotten some of the humiliations he had suffered at Blaze's hands in the past. Nor did he like the disdain with which Blaze was treating him now. But he tried to keep his rancor hidden.

"Don't forget one thing, you lizard-lipped *hombre*," Blaze said in conclusion. "You're to follow my orders. You'll be paid well for a job that offers little risk. Half of it will be in advance. Don't build up any ambitions about doing the thinking in my place. I'll stamp you out as I would a scorpion if you don't walk chalk. Savvy?"

"Hell, ain't I give my word?" Slate protested.

"Your word is good as long as the other man don't turn his back on you, Slate. I can out-shoot you for beans or blood, an' I don't intend to have a bullet cut my suspenders. Keep that in mind."

The next day Blaze rode north, accompanied by five followers whose presence caused his gorge to rise. There were two pockedmarked half-breeds who rode barefoot. The soles of their leathery feet showed the scars of the *bastinado* for past crimes. There was an unshaven renegade with a thin, wrinkled neck, who was said to be wanted for a double killing in Santa Fé, and a toad-bodied, snaggle-toothed desperado who smoked marijuana. And there was Tony Slate. . . .

They camped in the mesquite hills overlooking the rolling Rafter M range, and spent a few days learning the country. Blaze then sent one of the half-breeds with word to Travis Merchant that they were ready.

Tony Slate, who knew this range, located the Wishbone brand on the flats beyond Bowie Creek. Two cowboys were stationed at a line camp there, riding fence and bog. Blaze

had them watched each day. True to Merchant's promise, th
Rafter M cowboys were pulled out of that line camp for wor
elsewhere on the range.

During their absence, Blaze and his five men cut out six
big, fat steers, and trailed them ten miles farther north, dee
into the hills. In a hidden basin they worked with hot runnin
irons in the sun and dust, changing the Wishbone brand t
the Hourglass.

It was a simple matter of adding prongs and crossbars t
the Wishbone mark. Travis Merchant, no doubt, had reco
nized the possibilities of altering the brand, when he bough
up the Wishbone cattle.

"Half of the skunk work is done," Blaze commented whe
the last of the steers had been worked over. "I'm takin' a littl
pasear now. I'll be back tomorrow. An' we'll move 'em to ne
range. I'll pay you boys the other half of what I owe you ther
an' we'll part company for keeps."

"Just who's puttin' up the *dinero* for workin' over thes
critters?" Tony Slate asked casually.

"I didn't say," Blaze answered.

There was a wise glint in Slate's eye. Blaze discovered tha
Tony Slate was no stranger to this range. Slate knew all th
brands and the owners, and, although he never had men
tioned it, he probably knew of the old feud between Travi
Merchant and Joe Sealy. It was also common knowledge tha
Blaze's brother was in El Citadel, and Slate probably wa
aware that Travis Merchant was the brother-in-law of th
comandante. It should be no trick for Slate to piece these fact
together.

But Blaze was indifferent as he rode away. Slate's knowl
edge was none of his concern. Someday, perhaps, Slate migh
use it in an attempt to blackmail Travis Merchant. Blaz
grinned faintly. Merchant would have to kill his own snakes

Blaze aimed to see Merchant after dark. The Rafter M headquarters lay some fifteen miles to the northeast, out in the open flats away from the hills. The hour was mid-afternoon, and he rode leisurely north, following the hills for the sake of concealment.

Down on the benches, he sighted a roundup wagon, which had the Rafter M brand painted on the top. Travis Merchant evidently was cutting beef for market. Blaze swung deeper into the hills to avoid the circles that were being thrown out from the wagon.

It was twilight when he rode down to the flats. He cantered the remaining five miles to Merchant's ranch. Once more he tied up his horse and walked to the spread on foot.

The dreamy quiet of the patio gripped him powerfully. For the first time, he was aware of rankling regret for the wild life he had led.

Travis Merchant, smoking a black stogie, was in his den, reading a newspaper, with his spectacles canted far down on his nose. Blaze found the door unlocked and unguarded, as before.

Merchant laid aside the paper and removed his glasses as Blaze entered. He arose and drew the window drape. His gun now lay on the desk, within easy reach. He took his seat at the desk. He gestured toward a vacant chair, but Blaze Cardwell preferred to remain standing.

"Sixty head are ready," Blaze stated briefly. "I'm holding 'em back in the hills, not far beyond that flat-topped limestone ridge. What do you want done with 'em?"

Merchant drew a rough map. "Drive 'em north past Whitehead Ridge. That's the limestone ridge you mentioned. After about ten miles you'll come on a line fence on the red bluffs overlookin' Gooseneck Creek. Turn 'em out on the north side of that fence. That's all."

"Beef roundup is under way, I see," Blaze observe[d]. "Those worked brands will be discovered long before they'[ve] had a chance to heal. I've seen men hung on a hell of a sig[ht] less evidence than you'll have against the Sealys. Joe Sealy a[n'] his son will have to light a quick shuck to Mexico, if they'[re] goin' to keep out of Huntsville penitentiary. An' your skir[ts] will be clean. Your daughter likely won't ever know. A[n'] she'll learn to hate young Sealy, because she'll believe he w[as] snake enough to steal cattle from her father. . . . It's a sli[ck] frame-up, Merchant."

Travis Merchant reared to his feet. "Damn you, Car[d]-well!" he choked. "Hold your sharp tongue. It's toug[h] enough to have to stoop to this, without havin' you stan[d] there sneerin' at me. You're in this as deep as me. You'[re] doin' this to save your brother. I'm makin' a skunk of myse[lf] to save my daughter. Don't get any idea I'm enjoyin' it. I['ll] never be able to look an honest man in the eye again."

Blaze was startled. The bitter sincerity of the lean cowma[n] was unmistakable. "Why do you believe you're doing yo[ur] daughter a favor?" he asked harshly. "You can't rule a girl[']s heart."

"I've told you," Merchant growled. "Steve Sealy is onl[y] aimin' to marry her because his father has put him up to i[t.] Joe Sealy hates me. He was in love with the girl I marrie[d] twenty-five years ago. But she chose me. He never forga[ve] me. And he's brought up his own son to hate me, also. You[ng] Steve Sealy will make life a livin' hell for Amata, just to mak[e] me suffer."

Blaze shrugged. "Not knowing young Steve Sealy, I['ll] have to take your word that he's a skunk. It's none of my bus[i]-ness, anyway. I want that second thousand you promise[d] Merchant. I hired five buskies to help me, an' they've got [to] be paid off."

Merchant went to the safe, counted out the money, and handed it over. Blaze pocketed it.

"Now I want you to send word to your brother-in-law at El Citadel, asking a certain favor," Blaze said grimly. "I want you to write that now, an' start it south tonight."

Merchant shook his head stubbornly. "Not until the job is done. Not until the Sealys are run out of this range. I'm not taking any chances on bein' double-crossed by you, Cardwell. It runs in my mind that you'd swing over to the side of the Sealys the minute you knew your pals were out of El Citadel. Well, your job isn't finished yet."

Black storm clouds gathered on Blaze's face. He stood an instant, frowning and considering his course. Then he suddenly lifted his head, listening. Travis Merchant turned, too.

"Another fast rider comin'," Blaze continued with bleak humor. "Maybe it's Joe Sealy returnin' to finish what he started the first time I was here."

They heard the rider dismount and stride into the patio. But it was not Joe Sealy. The man who entered was a lank, bony-jawed cowboy. He shot a glance at Blaze, then addressed Merchant. "We caught a couple of brand-busters today, boss," he stated. "We was goin' to string 'em up, but the sheriff wouldn't stand for it."

Travis Merchant shot a quick glance at Blaze, and there was a chill of dismay in his eyes. "Who were they, Sam?" he demanded.

The cowboy answered triumphantly. "I reckon you could guess if you tried. Joe Sealy and his son, Steve. We got the deadwood on 'em. Found about sixty head o' Wishbones that had been spooked back into the hills an' run into Hourglasses. The brands had been worked only the last day or so."

Merchant's mouth was a thin, harsh line. He did not glance at Blaze again.

"Why wasn't I notified?" he rasped.

The cowboy looked puzzled. "It all happened too damn fast," he explained. "Long Shorty an' Pete Duveen found that some of them Wishbones had been run, when they went back to the line shack this mornin'. They come hightailin' to the roundup wagon down by Whitehead Ridge. I sent a cowboy to Latigo to bring Sheriff Murphy, an' the rest of us hit into the hills. We picked up the trail about noon, located the cattle in a big draw. There was evidence that four or five *hombres* had been there, but they must have seen us comin' an' hit a long lope for Mexico before we got within shootin' distance."

Sam was discomfited by the granite grayness on the face of his boss. "It was plain as day," he went on defensively. "The Sealys must have hired some rustlers to help blot them brands. The sheriff didn't waste no time goin' after 'em. He swore us in as specials, an' we moseyed over to their spread. Caught 'em both in, with nothing in their hands but forks loaded with grub."

"Where are the Sealys now?" Merchant asked hoarsely.

"They're in the calaboose in Latigo by this time, boss. The sheriff said it wouldn't be necessary for you to file charges ag'in' 'em. The Cattle Association will take care of that."

"And what did they have to say?"

Sam grinned faintly. "They accused you of framin' 'em, of course. They said us Rafter M riders must have blotted them brands. But we all got an airtight alibi. We've been workin' roundup for more'n a week, an' there's half a dozen rep men who kin swear that it was impossible for us to have done it."

Merchant turned away, and the wagon boss took that as his dismissal. With a puzzled glance at Blaze, he went out. An instant later a wild-eyed girl rushed into the room and confronted Merchant. It was Amata, the golden-haired daughter.

Her soft, young face was ashen. "Dad!" she sobbed. "I heard what Sam said. It isn't true! Steve isn't a cattle thief. There's been a mistake. You've got to do something."

Travis Merchant tried to take her in his arms. "Now, now, honey. Don't you get yourself worked up. It's out of my hands, anyway. The sheriff. . . ."

She thrust him away with a sudden blaze of fury. "You mean you don't *want* to help them!" she panted. "You hate them. You've tried every way you can to turn me against Steve." She pointed a shaking finger at him. "You did it," she half screamed. "You did set a trap for them. It's a frame-up . . . and you're behind it. My own father sending the man I love to prison! If you go through with this, I'll hate you to my dying day. Do you hear? Do you?"

Her hysterical voice broke. She began to sway. Blaze stepped forward, his arm going around her slender waist to steady her.

Consuelo Merchant, her eyes wide with dismay, came darting into the room, followed by her mother. Consuelo rushed to her sister.

"Take your hands away from her," she gritted at Blaze. With fierce strength, she almost tore the fair-haired girl from his arm.

Travis Merchant stood there, bloodless of countenance. But his deep-set eyes remained implacable as steel.

"Take Amata away, *querida mía*," he said to his wife. "She's excited and overwrought. Go with your mother, Consuelo."

Consuelo's angry words burned in Blaze's ears. Dully he watched her and her mother lead Amata Merchant back through the house.

VI

"GUNFIGHT VERDICT"

Blaze Cardwell looked at Merchant for fully a minute before he spoke. "What are you going to do about it?" he asked quietly, and the menace of death rang in his voice.

Merchant stiffened a little. "What can I do?" he said grimly. "It's out of my hands. You bungled it, Cardwell. You left a trail they could follow."

"You knew those cattle would be trailed," Blaze snapped. "You sent those riders back too soon"

"It's done. And it can't be undone."

"You promised that nobody would go to the pen for this thing," Blaze stated in a monotone. "You can undo that."

"I'll use my influence to. . . ."

"Hell!" Blaze exploded. He caught Travis Merchant by the throat, shaking him like a rug. "Influence? I want you to go into court and confess that you framed them. Understand?"

Still this implacable man refused to break or yield an inch. "Not by a damned sight! I'm going through with it. They deserve what they'll get."

Blaze's fingers tightened. "You're not fit to live."

Merchant's fingers clawed at Blaze's hands. "Don't forget your brother," he gasped, and even in that instant there was mockery in his voice.

Slowly Blaze's grip relaxed. He laughed hoarsely. It was more like a helpless sob. "You oily skunk," he breathed. "I can't kill you . . . not yet."

He thrust Travis Merchant away, and stood glaring at him for a moment in black bafflement. Then he turned and strode out.

For the second time, as he passed into the shadows of the old trees beyond the house, Consuelo Merchant stepped into his path and halted him.

Her hand moved. And he felt the hard nudge of a gun muzzle against his chest.

"I eavesdropped," she said tensely. "Don't move, Cardwell. The gun is cocked. I almost fired at you when you were choking my father. But I waited. I heard enough to convince me that you're behind what happened to Joe and Steve Sealy today. Talk now. Tell the truth. Why did you blot those brands?"

"Pull the trigger," Blaze said, and there was a lifeless note in his voice. "Damned if that wouldn't solve things for me, at that."

That shook her. After a moment she spoke again. "You were going to kill my father. But he said something about your brother, and that caused you to stop. I know your brother is in El Citadel. You're trying to force my father to have him released. Is that why you framed the Sealys?"

"I blotted those brands," Blaze said harshly. "Why I did it is of no concern to you."

"My sister's happiness is at stake. Amata will die of a broken heart if this thing goes on. I'll take you to the sheriff myself, and the law will force you to confess."

Blaze's hand snapped up, knocked the barrel of the .38 away from his chest. It exploded, and he felt a hot, numbing pain as the bullet seared a rib. He wrenched the gun from her hand.

"I promise you one thing," he panted. "No man will suffer for what I've done. No man except myself."

Suddenly, violently, without knowing why he did it, he caught her in his arms and kissed her, then let her go.

Men were shouting and running from the houses. Blaze turned and raced away through the darkness to his horse. He hit the saddle and swept on through the starlight, circling until he had shaken off the uncertain pursuit.

Blaze headed aimlessly for the hills again. The right side of his shirt was soggy with blood, which dripped down on the saddle skirt. He came to a creek, stripped, and attended the injury. The bullet had ripped a three-inch crease along a rib. He bathed it and contrived a crude bandage that checked the bleeding. It was not serious, but he would have a stiff, painful side tomorrow.

He rode on. After midnight he threw off in a little ravine where there was water and grazing for his horse. He lay stretched on his tarp for a long time, staring up at the stars, his mood somber. He had bungled this task, just as he seemed to have bungled his whole life. Instead of imposing his will on Travis Merchant, he was being used as a mere pawn to accomplish the rancher's relentless purpose.

His brother and Kaw Devers and Spoke Jessup had been in that musty tomb of El Citadel nearly two months now. It was said that each month in El Citadel aged a man a year.

At least, Blaze told himself, he still had the power to free them. Joe and Steve Sealy would soon be on their way to a Texas prison. When the stone walls closed on them, the gates of El Citadel would open for Ran and the others. Merchant had given his word that he would intercede with the *comandante,* once his own scheme had succeeded.

Blaze lay helpless, torn by remorse, hating himself, loathing Travis Merchant. He had to get Ran out of El Citadel.

The memory of Consuelo Merchant's vibrant allure in that brief moment he had held her, his lips against hers, arose to torture him with futile longing. And he kept thinking of that promise he had made to her — that no man but himself would suffer for his mistakes. It was a promise that, in justice to Ran, he could not keep. Like a yellow dog, he would have to sacrifice the Sealys to save his brother.

"The Sealys mean nothing to me," he argued aloud. "I've never even laid eyes on Steve Sealy. Likely Sealy deserves all he's getting."

Blaze saddled up at dawn. He decided to go to Esteros. There he would probably find Tony Slate and his renegades, awaiting the last installment of their pay. The money that Merchant had given him burned Blaze's pocket. It was blood money. He wanted to get rid of it as soon as possible.

But, as he headed south, following the hills, he came in sight of Latigo, the cow town and county seat, ten miles to the east, out in the rolling benches. From his lofty viewpoint, he could see an unusual stream of townward travel over the yellow, ribbon-like trails on the range below. Irresistibly Blaze was drawn to Latigo, also. He sensed that the trial of Joe and Steve Sealy was the magnet that drew the people of Latigo range to town that day.

It was past noon when he rode into the crowded cow town. The tie rails and wagon yards were filled. Ranchers had brought their families to town, with picnic baskets, to make a holiday of it. The bars were doing a roaring business.

Interest focused on the red brick courthouse overlooking the tree-shaded plaza. Groups of high-heeled, weathered men were gathered there and on the stone steps of the court building.

Blaze half expected to be recognized. He pulled his hat

low to help hide his flame-red hair, tied up his horse, and strolled into the crowd around the courthouse.

There came a stir and a craning of necks. He saw armed deputies coming from the little stone jail. They were escorting two prisoners to the courthouse.

Blaze saw the seamy, embittered face of old Joe Sealy. The stocky cowman wore a resigned, cynical expression. At his side stalked a six-foot, bronzed, clean-cut young cowboy, with sensitive mouth and quiet, dark eyes.

There was protest and shattered hope in Blaze's gaze as he watched young Steve Sealy and his father, handcuffed and guarded, mount the steps and vanish into the court building. Blaze had pictured a swaggering, shifty-eyed schemer. That was Travis Merchant's description of the son of his old enemy. Blaze knew the truth now. Merchant had lied, or his own hatred had warped his judgment. Young Steve Sealy had the earmarks of a man to ride the river with.

There was another swirl of interest. Blaze looked up dully. Consuelo and Amata Merchant were riding by, mounted on slim Thoroughbreds. The sisters were garbed simply in denim riding skirts, cool shirtwaists, and sailor-brimmed straw hats. The golden-haired Amata looked pale and worn.

Blaze instinctively stepped back, but he was too late. The dark eyes of Consuelo seemed to pick him out instinctively as he stood there in the shade of a granger's buckboard. He saw the shock of that discovery straighten her lips. Then she rode on by, without further sign of recognition.

The sisters dismounted, turned their horses over to a cowboy, and entered the courthouse. A bailiff came to the steps, began his "Hear ye! Hear ye. . . ."

Blaze turned and walked stiffly to a *cantina*. He stayed there, drinking steadily, as the afternoon dragged. The proceedings at the brand-blotting trial were relayed swiftly from the courtroom to the crowds in the street and in the bar-rooms.

It required more than two hours to select a jury. Unbiased jurors were not easy to find, it seemed. From the talk that passed around, Blaze learned that Joe and Steve Sealy were well liked in the Latigo country.

The trial started in mid-afternoon. Blaze stopped drinking. The evidence against the Sealys was damning, even though it was circumstantial. They had little defense. There was no support for their alibi that they had been at their own little ranch, ten miles away, cutting wild hay at the time the brand-blotting had taken place. The state had a long list of witnesses. The sheriff and his deputies, as well as the cowboys who had trailed the stolen cattle, were all heard in full.

Twilight came, sultry and dusty, over Latigo. Blaze remained in the *cantina* across the plaza from the courthouse.

"It's about over," he heard a cowboy say. "The judge is layin' out the law to the jury. Shucks, Joe an' Steve ain't got a chance. Maybe they are guilty, but it shore looks skunky to me."

Blaze straightened suddenly, left the bar. Early darkness was settling. He walked across the little plaza and mounted the steps of the courthouse.

The corridor was crowded. He shouldered through to the door of the courtroom. He stood there, looking down the aisle that the bailiffs had kept clear.

The Merchant sisters were seated in the front row, directly back of the two prisoners inside the enclosure. Amata Merchant's hand was locked in Steve Sealy's palm, across the low wooden rail.

The jury was standing. The foreman cleared his throat and began to talk. "I reckon, your honor, that it ain't necessary fer us to leave the jury box. We've reached a verdict. We find the prisoners guil. . . ."

Blaze moved a pace down the aisle between the crowded benches. "No!" he called out sharply. "You're findin' them innocent!"

He stood there, the center of shocked, staring interest, with every head turned toward him.

For the first time in weeks, the flush of his former, untamed, devil-may-care recklessness came back, full-blooded, into Blaze Cardwell's rugged face. "I blotted those brands," he said slowly, harshly. "The Sealys had nothin' to do with it."

The judge, gray-haired and stern, came to his feet. "Who are you?" he demanded.

Blaze's laugh rang jeeringly. "Blaze Cardwell, the border hopper," he rasped. "The outlaw the *rurales* believe they buried two months ago."

He saw Consuelo Merchant rise to her feet. She was staring at him with incredulous, shining wonder in her big, dark eyes.

"Do you realize that you're confessing a crime for which you will be sent to prison?" the judge demanded.

"You have my confession," Blaze mocked him. "I'm guilty! I was hired to frame the Sealys. But I can't go through with it."

"Arrest that man," the judge snapped curtly.

Blaze laughed, and then his gun was in his hand. "I'm not submittin' to arrest," he grated. "Stand back!"

He moved back to the door. The crowd opened for him, as men stampeded aside to avoid the menacing muzzle that roved hungrily. Blaze strode into the corridor, turned, and backed to the outer door. "Stay where you are," he warned coldly. He leaped through the door, raced down the stone steps through the press of puzzled bystanders, who turned to stare.

The two Thoroughbreds from Travis Merchant's prize

string stood tied at the rail. There was a rumble of alarm as Blaze vaulted into the saddle of the horse Consuelo had ridden to town.

Men surged toward him, but the menace of his gun halted them momentarily. Then he was on his way, using steel and leather. The Thoroughbred was covering ground in long strides before the first shot fanned Blaze's hat. Then he was among the trees in the plaza park, pushing the horse to the limit.

He sped across the plaza and into the darkness between buildings, as turmoil swept the town. The Thoroughbred held to a long, rushing pace for about two miles. When Blaze eased it down and listened, there was no evidence of pursuit.

He rode on toward the hills. The reckless zest had died from his eyes once more. He rode wearily. He had saved the Sealys; he had salvaged a remnant of his soul. But at what price? He had thrown away his only chance of opening the gates of El Citadel for Ran and Spoke Jessup and Kaw Devers.

VII

"RANSOM GIRL"

More than forty-eight hours later Blaze rode into Esteros. Somewhere on the trail he had helped himself to an ordinary cow pony, and turned free the flashy, easily identified Thoroughbred.

The hour was past midnight. Tomás Sanchez's *cantina* was almost deserted when Blaze stepped in. The fat, bland proprietor blinked at him in amazement, then came quickly to murmur a warning.

"The *cabrón*, Tony Slate, is near," he whispered. "He look for you. He say you . . . what you call eet? . . . double-cross him, yes. He will slip the dirk into your ribs, *Señor* Blaze."

"I didn't double-cross him, Tomás." Blaze shrugged indifferently. "Slide that tequila bottle nearer. I'm gettin' drunk tonight. Here's some *dinero* for Tony Slate and his *buchillos*. Can't blame Slate for accusin' me of it, but he's been wrong. He almost got caught in a fight, but it wasn't my fault. Give him the money. It's what I agreed to pay him. An' tell him to stay clear of me from now on. I'll never get the smell of him washed off me."

He tilted the tequila bottle. "Here's to hell, Tomás."

But the raw, biting tequila did not bring forgetfulness. The vision of grim old El Citadel, evil and impregnable, holding its black secrets like a bloated monster there on the bluff above Cabazón, burned always on Blaze's mind, torturing him.

He sat alone at a table in Tomás's *cantina* the next night, with a bottle in front of him. His face was haggard and strained, his nerves frayed to the breaking point.

The decision to go back to the Rafter M, for a final attempt to break Travis Merchant, crystallized in his mind. But in his heart he knew that Merchant would never break. He might kill Merchant, but he would never break the man with threats.

Tomás approached and, under the pretense of polishing the scarred table top, spoke to him: "I 'ave word that someone would spik to you, *Señor* Blaze. Go to the *cabaña* of my cousin, Pedro Silvas, the goatherder. It is not far. Fi' mile."

"Who is it?" Blaze asked without interest.

"My cousin bring thees, to give to you. It come from thees person who would have the *habla* with you, *señor*."

It was a folded scrap of paper. Blaze opened it. He stared

at the single name, written in a small, feminine hand. The name was Consuelo. There was nothing else on the paper. Blaze came to his feet suddenly, looking at Tomás.

"My cousin wait on the trail with the *caballos,*" Tomás murmured. "He do not wish to be seen."

Blaze found the *peón* and two saddled horses waiting in the darkness beside the trail just beyond the village. They mounted and rode over dim, crooked trails through the thorny pear and mesquite thickets.

The *cabaña* of Pedro Silvas was a rude, mud and straw-thatched hut in a clearing. The smell of goats was strong in the night as the two men dismounted. Blaze stood by his horse, his gun in his hand, wary of a trap, although in the past Tomás Sanchez had always been loyal.

Then his shoulders relaxed, and he slid the gun back into the holster. Consuelo Merchant, bareheaded, wearing men's Levi's, flannel shirt, and old, flat-topped hat and boots, stepped out from the shadow of the hut and came close to him.

"I feared that you might not come here," she murmured, her voice uncertain. "I was told that I might locate you in Esteros. Josefa, my Mexican maid, is the sister of Tomás Sanchez. That is how I found you."

"Why did you want to find me?" Blaze asked harshly.

"First, to thank you for what you did there in the court-room that day. That was brave . . . reckless, but brave."

"An' what else?" Blaze snapped impatiently.

"To tell you that three American prisoners will soon be allowed to escape from El Citadel," she stated softly.

Blaze took a stride nearer. His eyes were almost savage in their intensity as he peered at her in the starlight. "Explain that," he said hoarsely.

"What is there to explain? Your brother and his comrades will be released. Isn't that enough?"

"I can't believe you, *señorita*. Only your father could bring that about. And I have reason to believe that he'd walk through hell barefoot before he'd turn a hand to benefit me."

"You used the wrong tactics against him," she said huskily. "He has no fear for himself. Threats only make him more stubborn and hard. But the weapon that would bring him to terms was always there within your grasp. And you failed to use it." She paused. "You could have kidnapped Amata or myself," she went on, her voice a faint, shaky murmur. "That would have broken Travis Merchant."

Blaze uttered a short, disillusioned laugh. "I've fallen plenty low, but not to the point of stealin' girls." His voice broke off abruptly. He bent closer, glaring at her with sudden, tense disbelief. "You don't . . . ? Good God! You don't mean to stand there an' tell me you've . . . ?"

She straightened, her chin lifting proudly. "Yes! My father believes you have kidnapped me, Blaze Cardwell. I wrote a note, trying to make it look like a man's hand. I signed no name, but I made it clear that my ransom was the release of three Americans from El Citadel." She refused to wince, although Blaze's fingers had closed on her arms, biting into her smooth flesh. "By this time I'm sure my uncle, the *comandante*, has heard from father," she declared. "I stole away from home three nights ago. I am well hidden here with Pedro Silvas and his good wife. When you are certain your brother is free, I'll return to my father. Then, and only then, will I go back."

"Why are you doing this?"

"I owe you a debt, Blaze Cardwell. You prevented the thing that would have broken my sister's heart and ruined her life. This is the only way I knew to repay you. Your brother must mean as much to you as my sister does to me."

All the bitter, black hatred was gone from Blaze's heart as he stood there, looking into the girl's brave eyes. He spoke her name musingly, as though the mere sound of it was a soothing benediction. "Consuelo."

He turned away, but now she caught his arm, staying him. "Why did you say my name . . . that way?" she asked softly.

He looked at her. "I never spoke your name aloud before," he muttered. "It's a name I'll have trouble forgetting. Even an outlaw can't forget some things."

She was standing so close that the loose, rich strands of her hair brushed his cheek. "I don't want you to forget my name, Blaze Cardwell," she said steadily. "You may be an outlaw. They say you're untamed and reckless. But I'm proud to hear you speak my name."

Blaze drew away from her violently, turned, and mounted his horse. "I love you," he said harshly. "I've no right to say that, but I'm saying it anyway. You'll forget me someday, but I'll never be able to forget you."

"Blaze!" she choked, and her eyes were bright and moist in the darkness. But he could not see that. The *thud* of hoofs, as he nicked the horse and whirled away, drowned out her plaintive call.

He did not look back as he headed up the mule trail to Esteros. He never knew that Consuelo Merchant, half sobbing, half laughing, breathed his name over and over as she held to her breast her arms on which the marks of his fingers still showed. She stood there until the slog of hoofs died away, then sighed and went back into the hut, where Pedro Silvas and his wife were making her bed ready.

After she had gone to sleep, there was silent movement in the chaparral near the goatherder's shack. Two slovenly garbed men crept away through the thickets until they were safely beyond hearing.

It was Tony Slate's dry, rasping voice that spoke to his companion, a pockmarked half-breed. "Lucky we didn't dust that double-crossin' redhead on the trail, Chig. He's got it comin', for leavin' us there in that deadfall, hopin' we'd be caught with them hot cattle that day. But we've made us a chunk of money by holdin' off to see where he was goin' with Tomás Sanchez's cousin."

Chig was less imaginative. "What you mean?"

"Didn't you hear? That gal is the daughter of Travis Merchant, who's got plenty of *dinero*. Merchant will pay out good gold to ransom her. We're goin' to have the beautiful *Señorita* Consuelo Merchant as our guest on the trail, Chig."

Chig, the half-breed, flinched. "It is bad to steal women," he said in Spanish. "For this they sometimes make you die very slowly, very painfully. Gold will do us no good when the *señorita* returns to her father and sends the posses to hunt us down."

"I'm not such a damned fool, you wooden-faced pelican. The girl is too pretty to send back to her father. We will keep her with us for a while. Then . . . *quién sabe?* A missing girl can't talk. Blaze Cardwell is the man they'll hunt down. We'll git square with him, an' fill our pockets with gold at the same time. Here's the horses. Let's find Taz an' the other two boys. Five of us can handle this without any slip-up."

VII

"MURDER IN THE MESQUITALS"

Blaze returned to Esteros, Tomás Sanchez placed a tequila bottle on the bar as he entered, but he pushed it aside. Tomás eyed him, puzzled by the change that had come over the brawny redhead.

For the first time in weeks Blaze's sleep was untroubled by wild dreams of El Citadel as he bunked in Tomás's adobe shack at the rear of the *cantina* that night.

He spent the next day in thoughtful idleness at the *cantina*, drinking nothing, but rolling one quirly after another. Hope and doubt tore at him. . . . Hope that by this time his brother and Kaw Devers and Spoke Jessup would be free from El Citadel. Black doubt that Travis Merchant would give in, even to save his daughter.

Always the knowledge that Consuela Merchant, with her dark, soft eyes and proud loveliness, was so near to him, lay heavily on his mind. Vast longing tore at him. More than once he half arose, impelled to ride down to Pedro Silvas's hut. But he steeled himself against it. That would only intensify the emptiness and futility of his life.

The money intended for Tony Slate still lay unclaimed in Tomás Sanchez's iron safe. Tomás had sent *peónes* to find Slate, but they had returned with word that he and his followers were missing from their usual haunts.

"Keep it for a while, Tomás," Blaze said indifferently. "If they never come back, give it to your cousin, Pedro Silvas, and tell him to use it as a stake to make himself a rich goat rancher."

Balmy darkness had come again over Esteros. Blaze sat alone at a table in the *cantina,* trying to keep his mind on a game of solitaire, when a lone rider pulled into town and tied up at the rail.

Blaze looked up as the man entered, then came to his feet with a surge.

"Ran!" he blurted out, and he walked down the room to grip the hand of his brother.

Ran Cardwell's face was haggard and bleached from the

months in prison. El Citadel's scant rations had thinned and weakened him. "I don't know why or how it happened, Tom," he said hoarsely. "Four days ago, at midnight, me an' Kaw an' Spoke was taken from the cells, marched outside the prison. We figgered it was a firin' squad. Instead, there were horses waitin'. We rode to Laredo, where Kaw an' Spoke went on a roarin' drunk. They told me I might find you here in Esteros."

"It doesn't matter how it happened, Ran," Blaze said. "You're out of that hell-hole." He turned to Tomás. "Send word to your cousin that it is finished," he said in Spanish. "He will understand."

He looked to Ran. "You're tuckered, fella," he said. "That *cuartel* took toll. Tomorrow we're riding north. We'll go to Wyoming or Montana. I'm quittin' the border, quittin' the long trails. Forty a month is big money. . . ."

Blaze's eyes lifted, then narrowed and went hard and cold. Another man had stepped through the door of the *cantina*. He stood there now, crouching with cocked six-shooters in his hands. It was Travis Merchant!

"Lift your hands, Cardwell," he gritted. Merchant's eyes were burning brands, his face drawn. The steely self-assurance of the man had crumbled. He looked as if he had not slept for days. "Where is she, Cardwell?" he spat hoarsely. "Where's my daughter? Damn you, talk! I've done my part. I had your wolf pals freed from El Citadel. That was days ago. Where is Consuelo?"

"Consuelo is safe," Blaze said grimly. "Put down your guns, Merchant. She'll be in your arms inside an hour. Tomás, send someone to show this man the way to your cousin's *cabaña*."

Blaze started to turn away. A harsh growl from Merchant halted him. "No you don't, Cardwell. Stand where you are! An' keep your hands away from your guns. You're getting no chance to run until I see my daughter alive and safe. You're the man who will lead me to her."

There were a half a dozen tough, wanted men in the *cantina*. Blaze saw them edging back against the walls, their hands sliding near their holsters. Tomás Sanchez's arms had dropped out of sight behind the bar. Tomás had scatter-guns loaded and ready under the bar.

"Hold it, boys," Blaze snapped. "Keep out of this. I don't need any help."

A second man appeared in the door of the *cantina* with a gun in his fist. He stood behind Travis Merchant. He was tall, with quiet, dark eyes. Steve Sealy!

"I'll ante into any gun play that starts, Cardwell," young Sealy said grimly. "The favor you did for me don't keep me out of this. Lift your arms. You're going with Merchant. An' if Consuelo isn't safe, I'll kill you myself."

Travis Merchant shot a startled glance over his shoulder. "Damn you, Sealy!" he hissed. "Where did you come from? I'm asking no help from you."

"I've been trailing you, while you trailed Cardwell's brother all the way from Cabazón," Sealy said. "Consuelo happens to be my sister-in-law. I've been watching you ever since you got that ransom letter, knowing that you'd need help."

Merchant straightened, glaring at him helplessly. "You . . . you married Amata?" he panted.

"I was married to her more than a week before you pulled that frame-up on me and Dad," Steve Sealy growled. "We kept it a secret, hoping you an' Dad would come to your senses and forget that old grudge."

Merchant, with a savage, half-mad snarl, swung his guns to bear on Steve Sealy. "You sneakin' . . . ," he began.

Blaze leaped. He knocked the guns down. They roared and blew dust from the packed adobe floor. Then Blaze stepped back, with the rancher's guns in his possession.

"You're a poisoned wolf, Merchant," he grated. "You've let hatred rule your life and shrivel your mind. Your daughters love you, but you've done everything you could think of to turn them against you. Come to your senses before it's too late. I'll take you to Consuelo. I never kidnapped her. She'll tell you that herself."

Blaze turned and strode through the door. He looked at Steve Sealy. "You better come along too, Sealy," he rasped.

Blaze saddled his horse at the corral. Travis Merchant and Steve Sealy, mounted, waited for him in the street, and rode at his side as he loped out of Esteros into the dark trail through the mesquital.

They rode in utter silence, Blaze in the lead, with Merchant following and Steve Sealy bringing up the rear.

Pedro Silvas's hut was dark and silent as they rode up. Blaze halted his horse twenty paces away. A sudden, eerie premonition of disaster beat at him.

"Wait!" he said sharply, stepping down from his animal. He walked to the hut, guns in his hands.

Something shadowy and shapeless lay across the threshold of the goatherder's hut. Blaze paused, his veins running icy. Slowly he bent closer.

It was the body of Pedro Silvas. There was a rustling sound in the darkness of the hut, then a groan. A faint, agonized voice came: *"¡Ayuda! ¡Madre de Dios! ¡Andale!"*

The goatherder's wife lay inside the door, with a stiletto driven in her back. Blaze's hoarse shout brought Travis Merchant and Sealy.

The dying Mexican woman breathed a few words in Spanish. "They kill my Pedro, steal the *gringo señorita!* Tony Slate! They ride away toward . . . toward the Río. . . ."

She died before she could say more.

IX

"THE RÍO GRANDE RUNS RED"

Blaze lifted the bodies to the rude bed in the hut, laid them side-by-side, and covered them with blankets. He handed Travis Merchant the guns he had taken.

"We're riding," he spat. "They've got no more than half an hour's start on us. We can stop 'em at the river. They're trying to take her into Mexico."

They hit the saddle and fed steel to the horses. Blaze led the way.

"Who are they?" Steve Sealy asked.

Blaze laughed bleakly. "Tony Slate is a rat I hired to blot brands on some cattle up in the Latigo range a few days ago," he stated, and he was looking at Travis Merchant. "You see how chickens come home to roost, Merchant."

The sign of their quarry showed plainly in the dim wood-chopper's trail that Blaze followed.

After they had ridden for an hour through the blackness of the chaparral, the dank breath of the Río Grande met them. The mesquite and pear thickets gave way abruptly to swamp oak and willow bosques.

The horses were laboring and lather lay heavily on their flanks, but Blaze set the pace relentlessly. His fingers were wrapped around the handle of a gun as he rode. He prayed that Tony Slate would come within his reach. But he went sick at heart as he thought of the nearness of the river. If Slate and his renegades crossed it, they would have all of Mexico to lose themselves in.

Then, in the starlight, Blaze saw the glint of the river, coiling its dark, somber length through the swamps. With a groan, he eased the pace.

"Silence!" he warned suddenly, lifting in the stirrups.

All of them heard it then — the distant, foaming, splashing surge of wading horses.

"They're fording the river," Blaze said.

He hurled his mount ahead, plunged from the brush into full view of the muddy, dark river. Dimly he sighted scattered dots in single file almost halfway across the two-hundred yard expanse of water.

A rifle spat wickedly out there then. The bullet whistled past him. Blaze hurled his horse at full gallop into the shallow water of the ford. He did not look back. He was barely conscious of the fact that Steve Sealy was riding at his heels and that Travis Merchant, on a slower horse, was in the water, too, cursing like a madman.

Rifles were cracking viciously, the flashes coming from the water ahead, where the mounts of Tony Slate and his four men were down to their bellies in the river. Spray and water from the flying hoofs of their mounts soaked Blaze and Steve Sealy and blinded Travis Merchant.

Blaze felt the tug of a rifle bullet on his sleeve. "Hold your fire," he panted at Sealy. "Consuelo is there with 'em."

The renegades were forcing their horses, but they were almost in swimming water. The three pursuers steadily lessened the distance between them.

"Go back, damn you!" Slate's voice came, shrill and frantic. "Damn you, we'll kill the girl if you come any closer."

"If you hurt her, I'll take you alive and carve your hide to ribbons!" Blaze shouted. "I'm comin' to get her."

A slug drilled Blaze's cheeks, and a gush of blood and teeth spilled from his mouth. He forced his horse on. At fifty yards' distance he could make out the shapes of the five riders ahead. He marked the doubly burdened horse that carried Consuelo and Tony Slate. Then he cocked the hammer of his gun and began firing. He picked the lone riders as his target. He saw one saddle go empty. A horse, relieved of its burden, swung wildly, floundering downstream into deeper water.

The renegades, panic-stricken, were scattering, their bullets coming in a frenzied sleet. Slugs struck long spurts of water around Blaze and Steve Sealy; ricocheting, they screamed off into the night. Sealy's .45s were thundering methodically now. A second renegade, with a choked scream of agony, pitched from his horse. He splashed for a second or two as the current swept him downstream.

Blaze saw Steve Sealy reel in the saddle, clutching the horn an instant, then slowly, stubbornly draw himself erect and begin firing again. The distance was a short rope's length as Blaze blasted a third man from the saddle. And he heard the roar of Travis Merchant's guns behind him. The fourth rider had abandoned his horse and was trying to swim downstream. His head was a dim dot on the surface, but it vanished as Merchant's .45s roared.

Tony Slate, with Consuelo as his shield, remained there alone. Slate was using a six-shooter now, firing at Blaze, but his horse was staggering and floundering in water that came above the saddle skirts, and his aim was wild.

"Stay back!" Slate screeched as Blaze came surging relentlessly upon him.

He fired almost pointblank at Blaze, but Consuelo twisted and upset his sights in time. Then Blaze was upon him. He knocked Slate's gun spinning from his hands. Their exhausted horses went down. Blaze's fingers clutched Tony Slate's throat as they fell into the river. He felt Consuelo kicking and struggling against him, as the muddy tide closed over them.

For seconds Blaze held his grip. All the power of his body seemed to concentrate in his fingers and wrists. Then he released the thing that had been Tony Slate, consigning it to the river.

He felt Consuelo's long hair float against his face. His hand caught her before the current swept her away. He found footing, thrust his head above the surface, lifting the girl clear, so that she could breathe air again. Her wrists were bound.

He tore the gag from her mouth and staggered to shallower water. Travis Merchant, still mounted, lifted Consuelo from his arms. He dimly saw Steve Sealy drooping over the saddle horn as his panting horse turned and waded back toward the Texas shore.

Blaze felt himself reeling in the current, unable to fight his way back to shore. He vaguely realized that more than one bullet had found him.

"Blaze!" Consuelo called wildly. "Dad, help him! He's been shot. He didn't kidnap me. I ran away. Help him. I love him, Dad! Don't you understand? I love him!"

He saw Travis Merchant's horse turn. And then he was being pulled up on it.

"Help Steve," the girl panted now. "See! He's been shot, too. He'll fall into the river."

Her voice faded. Faintness gripped Blaze.

A hot morning sun was cutting away the river mists, when Blaze sluggishly aroused from his coma. Consuelo's face was bent anxiously over him. She smiled wanly. He caught a glimpse of Steve Sealy, white of face, lying beside him under a tree.

Travis Merchant, muddy, his clothes in tatters, grinned as Blaze's eyes lifted. "I reckon I better start to bring help now, sweet," Merchant said to his daughter. "It looks like that red-

206

head will pull through, too. That slug through his face will give him a couple of dimples. 'Most anything would improve his looks, I reckon."

Steve Sealy spoke. "You might send word to Amata . . . if it wouldn't be asking too much."

Merchant looked at him. "I'll do it, s . . ." he hesitated, and Blaze could see the battle between his pride and his humility. Then, with a growl, Travis Merchant thrust out a hand to Steve Sealy. "I was wrong," he blurted out. "I've been wrong for twenty-five years. I started to call you 'son', Steve Sealy. Damned if I ain't proud to call you that. Maybe one reason I hated your dad was that I never had a son."

And Travis Merchant, drawing the last tattered vestige of his lost austerity around him like a cloak, climbed onto a saddle and headed away to bring help from Easteros.

"Well, I like that!" Consuelo said, tears of happiness belying her tone. "I suppose a son is more important than a daughter."

Blaze caught her hand. "Not to me," he said. "I heard something last night, just before I passed out. Maybe I dreamed it. It sounded like an angel said she loved me. That can't be, of course. Angels don't fall in love with border runners."

Consuelo's eyes were gravely tender as she bent closer. "Not angels," she breathed. "I'm no angel, Blaze Cardwell. I'm a woman. And I love you, no matter what you are."

Steve Sealy, watching them, grinned. "Looks like Travis Merchant is goin' to have another son," he commented. "An' I got a sneakin' hunch he'll think a damned sight more of him than he does of me."

NIGHTS OF
TERROR
STEVE FRAZEE

The heart of the American West can be found in the Western fiction of Steve Frazee. This collection of eight short stories showcases Frazee's ability to produce suspense and excitement while capturing the past with impeccable historical accuracy and a deep understanding of human nature—including its dark side. In the title story, Frazee blends elements of a gripping thriller within a Western setting. Because of rustling, ranchers have taken to posting a guard at Big Ghost Basin. When three of those guards are killed, all the evidence points to a gigantic beast whose tracks match those of no known animal—a beast who's never been seen by anyone still alive!